God's Poker Night

A *"What If...?"*
Look at God

By

Leslie Baker

www.bookstandpublishing.com

Published by
Bookstand Publishing
Pasadena, CA 91101
4909_5

ISBN 978-1-953710-98-7

Cover Design by Leslie Baker
Cover Photo by Dusan Jovic – Unsplash

Disclaimer

The following stories are fictional and do not depict any actual person or event. Also, you will notice throughout that, while God's name is capitalized, I didn't follow the practice of capitalizing most uses of he, him, you, heaven or hell. After trying it, having all those capitals felt awkward and intrusive. No disrespect is intended in this decision.

It's kind of a matter of semantics. If one uses the word 'praying' to denote asking for divine intervention, he may be disappointed... unless luck steps in. But if he interprets 'praying' as looking to his soul, his wiser self, for calm and guidance, he may find the strength to handle whatever comes.

<u>God Helps Those Who Help Themselves</u>

This book is dedicated to Jonathan Pembroke
who not only did some great editing for me,
but pointed out how appropriate this old saying is to
God's Poker Night

In The Beginning

You are an intrepid soul! Not everyone is audacious enough to chance looking at God in an unconventional light. There's something in here to offend and amuse everyone; especially a brave creature like you.

God is portrayed in wildly out-of-the-ordinary settings. You'll find no disdain for anyone's religious beliefs, (skeptics get the same treatment as holy rollers) but a quirky reexamination of possibilities. I hope you'll enjoy a few laughs, too.

Atheist or Catholic, Mormon or Muslim, all I ask of my reader is that you suspend the need to defend your beliefs as you read this. It's fiction, have fun with it!

God's Poker Night is a series of very short, unrelated stories consisting of snippets of conversations between God and an assortment of believers, non-believers and hell-bound sinners.

Most of the stories take place in heaven while a few are of a person chatting with God from earth. The characters are, with the exceptions of God, Saint Peter and God's regularly scheduled poker group, unique to their one story, so don't feel you have to try to memorize them.

Enjoy!

First Commandment

You Shall Have No Other Gods

It was one of those deliciously stormy evenings in heaven when the snow and wind blustered ferociously outdoors but the cozy fire crackled through it all. What had begun as a poker game in front of the wide fireplace had mellowed into a gab session in leather chairs with hot toddies at hand.

Fausto had been slightly uncomfortable when the deck of cards he'd first pulled off the shelf, shuffled and dealt had featured an assortment of deities on the back sides as well as the faces. They were gorgeous to look at, but a little ouchy when playing cards with God. "Wow. No other Gods before you, huh? Should we scrounge up another deck? Easy to do if these are an annoyance."

As the unease showed around the table, God had brushed it aside, admired the artwork and easily taken the first pot. This group had a standing date for poker night here in heaven and a pretty good idea of God's philosophies, but they'd never before happened onto the subject of the Ten Commandments.

Now, enjoying the fire, Ruby returned to the topic; "So, you're not troubled by all of the other 'Gods' who have been worshiped over man's history? What became of those who idolized them?"

God sipped thoughtfully before answering; "Without doing an inventory, I'd say that most of those people are here. When they first arrived, they all saw me, as you did, as they had imagined their version of 'God.' Trust me when I tell you I've donned some wild get-ups to make each of you feel welcome and loved. And, no, Ruby, I wasn't troubled by what they believed; life is an evolutionary process and they were just working their way through it."

Fausto began; "If the very first commandment basically forbids other gods, how do any of those worshippers end up here? Is it just because... "

Carl's voice squeaked, he was so unnerved as he interrupted. "But a lot of those folks were into animal and even human sacrifices, weren't they? I mean, I can see that there might be some slack cut for those following Buddha or other peaceable leaders but throwing live people on pyres is as extremely wrong as it gets!"

"Well, Carl, Buddha is an interesting fellow, I'd like to see the two of you meet. But, as to those who committed atrocious acts in the name of their gods, you have to put it in the context of their times. No one was born knowing who I am or *how* to honor me, so every civilization had to muddle its way through. Their souls told them I *existed*, but that was about it. So you're right, awful things have always and continue to happen in my name. But a lot of wonderful acts are done in some other god's names, too. If their fellow man, in their own time, would not have found their actions out of the range of acceptable, then that's what informs most of my judgments."

The fire had been allowed to sputter down to a few glowing coals and the evening had been a stimulating one. As the four began saying their goodnights before heading into the now balmy, starry night, they chatted about possibly addressing the second commandment on their next poker night.

***

Leslie Baker

Do Unto Others

"Seriously?" The woman asked of the tsking prude behind the podium. "Honey, if I'd screwed all the guys I was rumored to have, I *still* wouldn't be able to put my knees together! "

"Well," sniffed Saint Peter, "it's not my job to judge, I'm just the gatekeeper. Have a seat and I'll let you know when he's ready for you."

Edna couldn't resist snarking: "Do you ask the same insulting questions of the *men* who pass through here?"

As Pete puffed up to deliver his reply, something caught his attention and he instead noted formally that she could proceed through the opening door.

"What a jerk." Edna was muttering to herself as she entered an Eden-like garden.

"Hmmm...Did you catch Peter on a bad day?" God asked soothingly.

"Ohmygosh! It's really you! I've kept thinking I was dreaming. I'm not, though, am I? Please tell me no; I'm so excited!"

God laughed heartily at such exuberance. "Well, Edna, I'm glad to see you, too! What on earth could such a bouncy person as you have said to pull Pete's chain?"

"Oh, he was looking at some notes when I showed up and we just got off on the wrong foot, I guess. He seemed to think I was the worst slut since the Whore of Babylon. He wanted to know how many men I'd slept with."

"Not really his place to ask, was it?" God asked rhetorically. "Obviously, we have the notes on everything from how many times you stubbed a toe to how many people you slept with, but it's *my* place to conduct welcome interviews; I'll have a word with him."

"Well, if that's on the list, let's just go for it." Edna smiled, "What do you want to know? My resume? My dating history? Don't you have everything?"

"Both your personal and professional resumes are impressive; so few things jumped out at me that, if not for this diversion caused by Peter, ours would have been a very short interview; I would have just escorted you through the gates with my best wishes. As it is, I'm glad we have a moment together, your excitement at being here is contagious." God was smiling broadly.

"So, you're not going to grill me about my romantic life?"

"It doesn't look to me like you lied, cheated or intentionally hurt people; at least beyond acceptable limits, so, no, I really don't need a rehash unless there's something that's bothering *you.*"

"I had a great life," Edna bubbled, "and I hope you know how grateful to you I am for it."

"You will be a happy addition, here, Edna. I know you have many friends and family members to catch up with and I hope you enjoy every minute." God smiled while he ceremoniously held open one of those pearly gates for someone who had made him laugh.

After smiling and waving Edna into her glorious future with the crowd of loved ones awaiting, God turned on his heel and stomped out into the vestibule where St. Peter's podium reigned. Pete looked up over the book he was reading and opened his mouth in greeting when he was stopped short.

"Goshdarnit, Pete! Why do you have to be such a jerk sometimes? Edna is a perfectly nice woman and did *not* deserve to have you be such a smart mouth. And, even if she *had* deserved it, that's <u>my</u> job, not yours!"

Coming down from the podium, Peter had the good grace to appear abashed and, in a rare conciliatory tone said "You're absolutely right. I regretted it almost immediately; don't know what got into me. I apologize."

With the wind taken from his sails, God harrumphed. "Fine then. But I'm not the one who deserves the apology, am I? Promise me you'll find a moment to say something kind to Edna."

"Oh, God. You know how I hate socializing; is that really necessary?"

Pulling rank as he seldom did with his old friend, God confirmed that it was. Patting Peter on the shoulder, God wandered back into his own room.

A few days later, Edna was toweling her hair after swimming laps when she felt a presence nearby.

"I'm sorry if this is an awkward time, would you prefer I contact you later?" Peter asked.

"Oh, it's you." Edna grumbled as she completed her towel turban. "I can't imagine we have much to say to each other, so just get it over with."

"I deserve that. There's no excuse for the way I spoke to you on the biggest day of your life. I sincerely apologize for having been such a rotter."

"Wow. Now *there's* something I never expected to hear! Your apology is accepted, Saint Peter. We've all had a bad day now and then and acted childishly, haven't we?"

"Please, it's just Pete. And I appreciate it. Your graciousness *does* make me look even worse, though, doesn't it?"

The two laughed and shook hands, bringing an awkward episode to a pleasing close. As she set off, Edna felt a rush of her customary optimism lift her spirits to new heights; life in heaven really is... heavenly!

***

Leslie Baker

<u>Whose Word?</u>

As God and Maury sat in heaven's wood-shop refurbishing some of the hundreds of tattered Mahjong tiles awaiting their turn, Maury began a rejoinder to God's comment with: "But, it says in the Bible..."

God laughed and told Maury that it's being the seventh day wasn't going to get them out of today's planned activity. "Nice try, though!" Chuckling, the two men settled back into their labor of love.

"I'd guess I'm not the first one to mention to you that you always seem to sidestep discussions of the bible, right?" Maury asked without looking up from his meticulous sanding.

"Sure, it comes up often and with varying degrees of pique." God was pleased to be treading this familiar path with someone as agreeable as Maury. "I've probably taken more abuse over the bible than any other issue. I've tried holding talks with good-sized groups to get everyone either on the same page or at least discussing it in a civilized manner, but I haven't been too successful. Beliefs learned from birth die hard."

"Well, I have heard you say that you don't have anything against the bible or most other religious books, but, for something that's your own word, you seem pretty lukewarm about it." Maury took a moment to whisk his tile lightly. "For instance, resting on the seventh day was your idea, so why are you so willing to set it aside?"

"How do you know that?" God asked.

"Know... what? That you said it? Because it's in the bible."

"How do you know *that?*" God persisted.

"Because I read it there from the time I was *learning* to read!" Maury's calm was fraying a bit.

"And you read it because a group of *men* wrote it.

"Now, I'm not saying it's a bad book or that any of the people involved in its production had nefarious intent; just that it isn't 'The Word of God.' The bible contains some good life lessons and guidelines, so there are certainly worse things to base your choices on, but it was written by man and is fallible. Golly, they couldn't even agree on whether Sunday is the first or seventh day of the week."

Maury stopped working entirely and gaped at God. "Are *any* religion's texts based on words directly from you?"

"No.

"From the time man first became aware of and struggled to convey his thoughts on me, he used whatever forms of communication were available to him: drawings on cave walls or stones, printed words, recordings, movies, memes, you name it. At each iteration, there have always been mistranslations, additions and omissions with or without malice. They are all man's words and there is no 'original' document that emanated from me.

"Even allowing for only the very best intentions, the bible is a flawed document. Its value lies in the unifying aspect it has. I would prefer that people trusted in their own souls as guidance, but I don't begrudge most 'sacred' tomes.

"What I heartily resent are the nonsensical edicts appended onto old texts by unscrupulous men who have used religion as a control device over needy and gullible portions of their fellows. Tell people what kind of underwear to don if they'll listen, but *don't* tell them that

I give a tinker's damn what they wear there, on their heads or around their necks!" God was as exercised as Maury had seen him.

After a few moments, God began again; "Wow. Quite the blow-up, huh?" He rumpled his hair with both dusty hands and looked sheepishly across the worktable at Maury. "I didn't say anything I don't believe, but I like to think I usually have a little more self-control than that. I apologize if I upset you."

Maury shrugged and allowed that he was glad God was comfortable enough with him to let off some steam.

"That's very gracious of you, Maury. You know, I'm happy for man to wear a shtreimel or a baseball cap, a mitre or a deerstalker. If it serves his purpose, I'm down with it. I just don't like having people prodded into believing *I'm* into one style or another. That they'll gain favor with me by following some mortal man's strictures."

By then, the afternoon had wound down and the two men began tidying the workshop. The peaceful camaraderie of the process was a soothing way to end the day.

***

Surf's Up!

"Dad! Dad!! Over here - I've got your board!" The healthy, tan young man loped across the beach with a surfboard under each arm just as the new arrival stepped away from the pearly gates. The vast, blue ocean twinkled under bright sunshine and the warm sand glistened. What a day!

What a day to be reunited. And, where better than heaven? The trials of ninety-five years of living lifted from the father's shoulders as he reveled in the sight of his long-dead 18-year-old son racing toward him.

The man glanced down and saw the trim brown body of his own athletic young self; the man his son would have known. From the moment he'd entered Saint Peter's waiting room, there had been no aches or pains, no hospital gown; only glorious health and freedom of movement.

The boy had long since forgotten the horror of his own last moments on earth as he died in the Korean demilitarized zone. He had arrived in heaven many years ago to the open arms of great-grandparents and cousins who introduced him to generations of family and friends he'd never met. As time passed on earth, more and more of those he'd loved there had arrived, and life was grand.

Never grander than this moment, though. The sight of his beloved father standing on the beach with an air of momentary confusion around him thrilled the son as never before. There stood his mentor in every sport a boy could dream of and in how to be a man. How to be a decent, responsible person willing to give his life for his country; a man like his dad. After the brutal foreshortening of his earthly life, the boy had been heartily welcomed to heaven by a loving and proud God all those years ago.

But no one, not even God, was prouder of his son than the man on the beach. That pride had not helped a whit with the almost unbearable grief which had persisted for the remaining years the man had been allotted on earth after the death of his son. The man's had been a good, happy and healthy life, but it always took only a word or a glimpse to cause a piercing stab of pain at the loss of all the potential taken from his son.

All the grief was suddenly gone, and the joy God had promised in his meeting with the man as he entered heaven was before him.

After an endless day of catching perfect (and some not-so-perfect) waves, the two tousled men flopped into a secluded cove.

"Aren't you ready to meet up with the rest of the family, Dad?" The boy searched his father's face.

"Oh, Sal, let me just look at you for a few minutes. In my wildest dreams of heaven, it was never this good; all my prayers are answered. I guess I'm feeling selfish; I want you all to myself for a while." The father smiled through tears and reached to cup his son's cheek.

The two men luxuriated in the sun and each other for a time before walking arm in arm to heaven's beachfront gathering spot where more joyful reunions awaited.

***

Leslie Baker

God Helps Those Who Help Themselves

"Is that going to help?" Curt didn't look up from the 2x6 chunk of lumber he'd almost obliterated with a framing hammer. Otherwise, his workshop was a tidy one.

"Well, it sure as hell can't hurt." Curt snarled as he hurled one more blow.

"You don't seem too surprised to hear from me." God intoned from Curt's soul.

"No." Curt set the hammer aside and pitched the mangled wood into a pile of similarly disfigured chunks. Yanking off his safety goggles, he snapped: "No, I figured you'd show up sooner or later to tell me what an ass I'm being."

"Why don't you sit down?" God sounded calm and reasonable, and, really, what choice did Curt have?

After a long and calming silence, Curt noted that taking out his frustration, anger and fear on an inanimate object he'd stockpiled for just this purpose, and recycled as firewood, seemed like the best he could do with those emotions. "I don't want to charge through the house like a banderillaed bull destroying the things she loves, and this sure as hell isn't the time to hit *her* for the first time ever. She's like a puppy or a little kid, she has no clue what she's doing or putting me through. My wife, my Alison is gone." Curt was on the verge of tears.

"No, she doesn't know you or what she's doing to you." God empathized quietly. "Dementia is so much kinder to the one *with* it than to the one *living* with it. I wish that scientists and doctors would do their jobs rather than pretending that all of their 'treatments' were doing any good at all. "

"Well, jeez, man, you're *God.* Aren't you the one with the final say? Can't you *make* them do the right thing?" Curt's voice had climbed in volume.

"You'd think so, wouldn't you? But, with earthly things, all of you are pretty much out of my control. The reason you have free will and reason is so you'll have the tools to determine your own destiny. That applies whether you're thinking about a third piece of pie or of murdering the guy down the street. You have to find ways to make appropriate choices."

"Yeah?" Curt sneered. "How's that working out for you? This world is such a mess that you can't be very satisfied with what's going on in it. Was it ever any better? Was there ever a time when people's brains worked right on a reliable basis? And, I mean, couldn't you take a mulligan, a do-over and get it *right?* What are you doing here right now if you can't do one damned thing to make our lives any better?"

God considered the desperate question for a few moments. "Regardless of rumors to the contrary, I don't have a magic wand. But I do have a heart, I do love both you and Alison and I can see that you are on the brink of making a poor decision. Not that you don't have a perfectly logical reason for doing so, but it won't help you, Curt. Shooting Alison and yourself could separate the two of you for all eternity, you could lose all hope of a healthy, joyous reunion in heaven. And Heaven *is* perfect; it gives you challenges when you want them, hammocks and beer when that's what you want, but it's *your* choice, your vision, right that moment, of 'heaven.'

"Hell, on the other hand, isn't something you want for yourself. If you end up there, 'eternity' takes on a whole new meaning. There is no mercy, no day off, no fishing hole. While there are a few murderers who have made it to heaven, it's a very fine line and not a good gamble to take."

"So this is as good as it gets, huh?"

"For a while, I'm afraid so. But you could make things a little easier on yourself by taking some of your neighbors, and your kids, up on their offers of help. People aren't very good at knowing how to offer the right *kind* of help; but if you'll ask the neighbors who have offered to lend a hand to take turns staying with Alison for, say, one Thursday afternoon a month, you could have *every* Thursday afternoon to yourself. Play nine holes with your friends. You'll be amazed at how much just that little bit of breathing space will help your outlook. The kids could alternate cooking Sunday dinners and stay current on Alison's condition.

"Curt, as you're seeing, you can't do it all yourself. You need to give people exact things they can do, and they will be there for you."

"This seems like such mundane planning for you to concern yourself with," Curt marveled to God.

"The big picture is made up of millions of tiny brushstrokes. I can't help with every one, but I hate to see a masterpiece go unfinished." smiled God as he melded back into Curt's soul.

***

The Worst Part of the Job

"So," boomed God, "you're the guy who raped those little girls?"

The fellow glanced over his shoulder at the subdued bar-scene, snapped his head back and snarled: "Yeah? What about it? Who the hell are you?"

"Answer my question."

"Not that it's any of your business, you old coot, but, yeah, I had a little fun with some girls who thought they were too damned good for the likes of me. Had to kill the one smart-mouthed little bitch who bit me, but the others lived to tell about it."

"How did *you* die?" asked God.

"What the hell are you talkin' about? I'm standing here waiting for a beer, just like you are, you senile old man. Dead. You're nuts, mister; move outta my way."

"So, you don't remember pulling a gun on that guy who confronted you about one of his daughters? He wasn't interested in a beer, as I recall."

"Mister, that wimp..." The guy paused, looked around and tried to gather his thoughts. "... Where *is* the wimp with the attitude?"

"He's having a pretty friendly chat with the policemen out on the sidewalk. When you drew on him, an off-duty cop took you out and saved the guy's life."

There was a long silence as the confused fellow began to put two and two together. He patted his hands down the flannel shirt and felt not much there.

"So...you...you're...God? Is that what's goin' on here?"

"Bingo. You're a pretty bright bulb, after all." God ended the interview by pushing down on a lever that released the squealing trap-door the heinous pig was standing on.

So, yes, even the worst of the worst sinners get to see God's face. But then, there's a long, dark drop down into the hell they've earned.

***

The Preacher and the Kid

"Oh, yes, you're the guy who wrote a weekly religion column for your local paper, right?" God continued in his conversation with the 67-year-old. They were wandering along, trying to enjoy the calm, oceanside setting in heaven.

Due to the circumstances of Harvey's arrival, God had arranged for Peter to escort him out to this spot where the two men could keep moving if they liked.

Harvey felt he was on pretty firm ground, metaphorically speaking, since he'd been a preacher for all of his adult life. God had, when first addressing him, been very sympathetic to Harvey's confusion and shock at having arrived in heaven so abruptly. The two appeared to start out the interview almost as colleagues.

"Yes, I lived in a rural, conservative area, so the paper always had two or three pages devoted to a couple of the other local ministers' writing, my column and a full page listing when and where all of the church services in ours and the neighboring towns were held. My parishioners were a vocal bunch and never held back on what they thought of that week's post!" Harvey was able to laugh as he remembered a few of his most outspoken members.

"As much as they may have ribbed you, it was obvious from the turnout at your funeral that you were highly thought of." God paused, knowing that, even with heaven's swerving timeline, the idea of his ghastly death hadn't quite reached full mute in Harvey's mind. When he suggested they take a seat in a couple of rustic chairs tucked into a cove, Harvey nodded.

There hadn't been much left of Harvey inside the nice (closed) coffin. The old refurbished, gas-powered wood-chipper had been donated to his church after Harvey proposed that the congregation could do the clearing for their new building and parking lot. They'd have lots of fresh mulch for flowerbeds and everyone could help. No one had mentioned the old chipper's disabled cut-off mechanism and, when he fell in, Harvey had been quickly dispatched.

Gulping with the memory, Harvey allowed that, yes, they'd been a generally great group. "If you already told me this, I apologize for being so rattled, but why did you have me die that way?"

"Well, Harvey, that gets us back to your column in the paper. I can't imagine you ever noticed how many times over the years you used phrases such as 'God wants...' or 'God says...' or 'God's plans for us...' did you? Now, I know you meant well and were trying to make me relatable to your people, but how did you know these things?"

After a thoughtful pause, Harvey began trying to put together an answer. "I was raised with and became a proponent of fundamentalist Christianity. You obviously know that means unwavering belief in the bible as your word and as our guiding principles. So, I guess I probably do begin a lot of sentences that way, though I wish some editor had pointed out the redundancy to me."

"The bible, whichever version a person reads, and the ten commandments are decent guidelines for life, Harvey, but they're man's thoughts, not mine. And I have no control over what happens on earth, certainly including your gruesome death..." God was unprepared for Harvey's vehement interruption.

"*Blasphemer!!* How can you say such a thing?!" The suddenly exercised Harvey began to realize what he had said and to whom. "How... what...I, I..."

"Shhh. It's okay, Harvey, you've had a lot to absorb recently and this conversation might have been better had at another point; I apologize for upsetting you." God was at his most calming.

After a long, settling silence, Harvey began hesitantly; "Believe it or not, I've suspected as much for many years; about your influence on earthly matters, anyway. There was never any way for me to address it even to myself, forget with my congregation or in the newspaper column.

"When I was a young pastor, I had to console an even younger couple in the death of their toddler. That baby was, besides being adorable, the whole world to his parents. It was a calamitous accident for his uncle to have backed a tractor over the child; none of it made any sense and the pain was just unimaginable.

"As I mentioned, I was pretty young myself and tried to explain it away, to all of us, as the will of God and tried to make it sound like you wanted Buddy here in heaven because he was so darned special that you just couldn't wait.

"Over the years, I faced innumerable times of helping my people through tragedies of all sorts. And there was never a time when Buddy wasn't there with me. His death was an enigma to me, and I was afraid, genuinely afraid, to try to make sense of the contradictions. How could I be preaching about this merciful, heavenly father while trying to brush aside the abhorrent things he inflicted on those who believed in and prayed to him?"

God reached over and patted Harvey's knee. There was so much, yet so little he could say to this good man who had felt an unutterable truth in his soul. "Harvey, you came so much closer to the truth than most people will allow themselves to even contemplate. I suspect your transition here will be less fraught with questions than those who *never* questioned."

The two rose and continued their walk enjoying the gentle air and camaraderie of two who were on the same page.

Weeks later, God made sure to check-in with Harvey to be sure that the transition to heaven had smoothed out for him. "*There* you are! And looking pretty buoyant, too!" God greeted the pastor as they walked through a park from different directions.

"I'm so glad to see you again!" Harvey's smile was a big one as he shook God's hand; "I *am* buoyant! In spite of the rocky initial metamorphosis, I'm just thrilled to be here."

The two men took a few minutes to climb and settle themselves at the back of the low bleachers overlooking a baseball field being used for a school-aged team's practice.

"So, tell me about a couple of your favorite reunions, Harvey."

"Well, of course my parents and grandparents are here and made the transition so much easier for me. My dad and I had always been edgy with each other, but it was wonderful to find that all those rough edges had been smoothed away. I guess we have the kind of relationship now that we'd both always wanted. What a gift.

"The biggest surprise was finding Julie, the girl I'd been engaged to when she was killed in that plane crash years ago. She and her parents, who died at the same time, have resumed their friendship with my folks and it's sort of exciting to be 'courting' again after all these years." Harvey actually blushed.

"I'm so glad to hear it, Harvey. You deserve all the happiness you find here.

"I wanted to point out another old connection that I don't think you've had a chance to make yet. See that fellow coaching the team in the field out there?"

"Sure, early-forties fellow? He doesn't look familiar, though, should he?"

God took a moment to ease into this. "Harvey... that healthy, community-minded fellow is our grown-up Buddy."

A sharp intake of breath and wide eyes greeted this news.

At the same moment, the coach called the practice and waiting dogs and other kids swarmed the field as the coach started up the bleachers toward God and Harvey. An enthusiastic hug and much backslapping ensued.

"Buddy! You've been a part of me for all these years," Harvey was sputtering through tears as he absorbed all of the implications. "Your mom and dad and at least one of your sisters were there when I died! Oh, they're going to be overjoyed, as I am, to see you when they get here!"

"Well, Pastor, I had a magical childhood here in heaven, and I'll be thrilled to see them, too, when the time comes. We are all so blessed to have a God" he turned his big smile on God, "who made such intricate plans for our earthly hereafter. I swear, I can't remember ever thinking: 'if only...' he thought of everything!" Buddy laughingly pointed to the kids and dogs tearing around the field, "See that green grass, Pastor? Who but our God would have had the forethought to eliminate elimination? No dog piles! Ever! You, Pastor will remember my Uncle Les and not be surprised to hear he's the one who pointed out the ingeniousness of it to me when I was old enough to see the significance. I didn't even remember them, but it's one of the first things newcomers notice." Turning back to God... "Am I right?"

Rumpling his hair like a schoolboy, God laughed and allowed that it *was* a favorite feature.

With laughter, the three men descended the now empty bleachers and walked into the gloaming to continue the conversation over dinner.

The small group claimed some seats at an outdoor cafe and continued their chat. The preacher was the one to bring up Buddy's uncle Les. Looking in God's eyes rather than Bud's, Harvey asked tentatively; "So Les really is here, is he? I'd have been afraid to ask because of the, um, circumstances of his death."

Both men looked to Bud for tacit permission to go further.

"It's okay," Bud said, "Uncle Les has been very open with me about, not only his suicide, but all of the conflicts he dealt with in having accidentally killed me and in knowing what one more death would do to our already devastated family. I'm so very grateful to you -" Bud looked to God "- for the mercy you showed to Les, and to us all, for not letting him go to hell for killing himself. I guess everyone on earth has a breaking point and having killed his sister's child was Les's."

God sighed and noted: "Suicide is always a fraught topic. Everyone views it as an unforgivable sin, but unless you've been in the kind of despair that makes it look like the only option, it can't really be judged as a stand-alone act. The totality of a person's life has to be looked at, and Les was a hardworking, family-oriented young man. With no wife and children of his own yet, Buddy's death really felt like the end of the world to him.

"Bud, it looks to me like your uncle Les has been one of your favorite surrogate fathers, is that right?"

"Oh, for sure!" Bud responded, "He got here so soon after I did that seeing him was fantastic. I was so little and, even though I had great-grandparents and lots of other people making over me, I didn't recognize their faces, Les's was the first one I really knew.

"It's funny, though, and I don't know that it ever dawned on me before, but even though I'd not known my great-grandparents on earth, I *knew* them. They immediately *felt* like family.

"Heaven's a great place for families. I've heard so many friends say that all of the conflicts are resolved before you even get here and you can really enjoy the best things about each other."

Just as Bud finished speaking, their meals arrived and the three men dug in.

***

<u>Sisterhood</u>

The two old friends sat on the enormous bed in a glamorous, if frayed, master bedroom suite. Their legs were crossed and they were surrounded by stacks of magazines, measuring tapes and yellow legal pads.

"Is this fun or *what?*!" enthused Leanne, "Just think of all the years when we were both doing this kind of work at the same time and never got the chance to do it together!"

Bouncing her bottom on the bed, Lisa smiled from ear to ear. "No kidding! How many times did one of us call the other one for thoughts and a fresh perspective on how to handle a window treatment or an awkward transition in a floor plan? I'm just flabbergasted that God would have arranged this for us and hiking trails for Karina! He thought of everything; he's really something, isn't he?"

"So much more than I ever dreamed. I was afraid that, *if* I got here, he was going to pat me on the head, give me a breather and send me back to earth to get it right. Mercy,

I was dreading that. I kept trying to put a smiley face on it, but, by the end, I was so exhausted I couldn't imagine starting all over again."

Lisa reached over and laid her hand on her oldest friend's hand. "Those last couple of years were so hard on you. And on everyone who loved you."

The two women had been childhood friends who stayed each other's closest friends, along with Karina, who was not into ratty houses and was out climbing mountains today, throughout all their lives. After their respective weddings in their '20's, hundreds or thousands of miles had always separated the three of them. They'd made a dedicated effort to stay connected through shared vacations, frequent phone calls and really making the commitment to not let these most important friendships drift away. One of Lisa and Leanne's most enduring connections had been a shared love of moving and of preferring old houses with character. Between them, they had revamped houses of every description, but never together.

"But now! Now we have the chance to strut our stuff, don't we?" Lisa was thrilled to be embarking on a project with someone whose tastes closely mirrored her own and whose opinion she respected. "Are we the luckiest women alive, or what?" she giggled.

Leanne concurred and noted that the three women, always united in their belief in God, now shared the joy in finding him to be even better that they had imagined. "And, you know one of the kindest things he gave us all? The ability to see the Karina or the Lisa we have in our hearts. None of us see the ravages of age when we look at each other; I see you two in bikinis on the beach the way we looked in our '20's, before melanoma destroyed our skin. What a gift."

After a long pause Leanne spoke again in a more somber tone. "I'm glad we all got here so close together, I know you and Karina were ready, too. And now, no matter how or when my sisters get here, my *real* sisters are with me."

"Oh, honey, your sisters were pretty good at the end. Even Marge flew in for the last few days, which I know you hadn't expected her to do. I'll bet that, by the time they get here, you'll be anxious to see them, and things will be all smoothed over. Don't you think? Really?"

Again, Leanne took a long time to answer. "Well, you're right that everything is kind of glossed over here in heaven, Even I don't feel the same level of animosity toward those two as I did, so maybe it really will be just hunky-dory. But... were you there when Sally spent that day helping me get my hair washed and rolled a few days before I died? She could *not* help herself! She brought up all that old stuff again and, if I hadn't been damned near dead, I'd have dragged *her* head under the water!" They both burst into laughter.

"Oh, you guys! Between you and Karina, I've always been *sooo* grateful to not have sisters! All of our brothers were nice guys, but you two and your sisters spent most of your lives at each other's throats. Of course, if any of you ever needed anything, the sisters rallied 'round, but there was usually a price to pay. I always felt lucky that you and Karina and I had all the perks and none of the aggravations of a 'sister' relationship!"

Laughter bounced the bed and their tools again. Yes, the softening would probably take place and there were always those hundred-year naps to fall back on if needed in coping with sisters.

***

Second Commandment

You Shall Not Make a Carved Image

Ruby was in high spirits after having whipped the three guys at the poker table; "Hey, when you're hot, you're hot!" she exulted as she flopped into the cushions of the down sofa.

Fausto arrived with Ruby's drink in hand and made a sweeping bow as he presented it to her "Yes, Ma'am, you *are* the winnah!"

Carl and God trailed behind lamenting the fact that they didn't have a rotating trophy of some sort for games like this one. "Oh, here!" enthused God as he swept a figurine of a Hindu goddess with many arms from the sideboard. He presented it to Ruby with a flourish while they all laughed and settled into their chairs.

As the giddiness began to subside, Carl picked up the carved figure from the coffee table and asked who she was.

"Like Ruby here," began God, "Durga is a warrior goddess. It's a beautiful piece of work, isn't it? I believe it's carved from some variety of Banyan wood."

"I'm kind of surprised to see ol' Durga here," Carl intoned, "doesn't she fall into the carved image category? You know, like in the second commandment?"

"Oh, pshh, that's an exquisite work of art. I'm saddened that people have been brainwashed into thinking I have so little self-confidence I'd feel threatened by an image of a goddess in an ancient religion." God scrutinized his children as he gauged how they would react.

"Now, that's the same logic I keep hearing from you on many topics. You often refute things most of us had hammered into us from bible school forward."

Fausto asked, "Why do we have so many things wrong on earth? And you say there isn't any way to correct them?"

"No, I can't correct those ideas until you get here," began God, "and even then, people have to be in the right frame of mind to feel comfortable putting aside foundational teachings. There's no hurry, though, and if, as happens fairly often, people are just more content with *not* changing their minds, there's certainly no pressure to do so. I want my children *happy* to be here, not feeling persecuted."

"How would you have reacted if one of us had fallen down and groveled before Durga?" Ruby asked. "That would fall into the category of 'worshiping an idol.' wouldn't it?

God laughed uproariously, "Well, if one of *you three* had behaved like that, I'd have thought the DTs had set in! Oh, what a picture..." He took a moment to regain his dignity before continuing.

"There are a still few religions on earth wherein idol worship is practiced, but I certainly don't take it as a personal affront. And, more importantly I don't damn people to hell for doing what they've been taught from birth was the right thing to do. Eliminating statues and images from religions could cause many of the most exquisite buildings and artwork on earth to be bulldozed in the name of the second commandment. Which sure wouldn't serve or honor me in any way, would it?"

"I wonder how long I'll have to be in heaven before I understand it all?" Carl voiced what the others were thinking as they tidied up and called it a night.

***

The Facilitator

Marla was all but banging her head on the wall when she heard, "What now, girl! You've been wailing and rending your clothes for days, but you don't tell me what I can do about it."

"But... but... you're God. If you don't know how to fix this, who does?"

"My job isn't to wave a wand and make your life perfect, Marla. My job is to facilitate. If you won't think your problems through enough to help me help you, then I can't do much. Give me something to work with, here."

"Lord! My mama's dying, my daughter's taken up with a bum and the roof's leaking. Where the hell do you want me to start?!"

"I'm in the middle of a poker game; let's talk again when you've gotten ahold of yourself."

"What's ... poker? In heaven? What the hell kind of place are you running up there?"

"Oh, girl. Heaven is different than you imagine it. Right now, as we have this chat through your own soul, your daddy and the Reeves' are saving your mama's place over at the bridge table while every old hound your daddy ever loved is flopped all around him. And... Dang! Look there! Now your daughter's bum of a grampa-in-law has just taken the pot while I'm lollygagging around with you!

"I'll let up on the rain for a day or two," God offered while glancing at the weather report for Cincinnati," but fixing that roof is on you. Don't be nippin' at me again until you have a good strong chat with yourself. We're in this together, girl, I can't do it all."

***

Out of My Hands

"I hung in there for as long as I possibly could at that hospital." answered the newly healthy old woman to God's question.

"Well, I was really referring to the last five years, not the last ten days. Your quality of life has been abominable since your first cancer surgery ten years ago." God gestured for her to have a seat across from him. "Why didn't you just come home then?"

"When I was seventy? I don't understand where you're coming from; how could I have died then? I don't mean to be evasive, but I just don't see what you're asking."

"Oh, I'm sorry," sighed God. "Yes, I know we're talking past each other. It's dispiriting for me to see so many people like you who lived good lives, contracted a fatal disease and then consented to torture for years afterward.

"Of course," he continued, "no one looks at it that way. The doctors and scientists feel that they're doing good work by prolonging life at any cost while patients and their families grasp at straws because it's become second nature for most of them to endure to the end."

"But," asked the confused woman, "if you think it's time for someone to die, why don't you just pull the plug yourself? Isn't it always your decision, anyway? If you don't like all of the surgeries and medications, why did you allow their development?"

"So many people believe I make all the decisions. They pray to me for the casserole to have not bubbled all over the microwave. For their favorite team to win or their old car to make it one more year.

"Frantic parents pray to me for a baby to live and thank me profusely when she does. But they rarely put together the facts that *their* baby girl lived while a hundred other babies with feverishly praying parents died all over the world in the same moment, leaving *them* raging in anguish. Who do they think does all of that picking and choosing? Me?" God sounded slightly pleading as he asked what he'd thought would be a rhetorical question.

"Um... well, yes. That's exactly what most people, at least those I know, believe. We all think that not a drop of rain falls nor a leg is broken unless you OK it. Are you saying that's not the case?"

"Yes, that's what I'm saying. Even if I wanted to, (and who could be *that* crazy?) that's not how it works. I created earth, man and beast, that's true. But with all the uncounted trillions of interactions among those entities and their offspring in any one nano-second, how could any one being control it?"

"Because you're God?" she asked.

"Yes, and many of you pray to me for blessings or in gratitude without thinking how contradictory it all is." It took God a moment to continue. "Let's say you've got two equally decent families living side by side in a leafy subdivision or a slum in Kenya; what would motivate me to inflict one family with a child's deformity, the father's economic ruin and the wife's cancer? While blessing their neighbors with robust health and endless financial success? Why would I be so inequitable with any blessings that were mine to bestow? What could possibly motivate me to such randomness?

"Why would I torture vast areas and all of the inhabitants therein, with flood, famine and fire? What kind of justification could there be? And yet, it's all chalked up to 'the will of God.' Yes, I created the earth. Once. And it's taken the course it takes as every aspect of it has evolved. But *man* is the creator of his own destiny.

"Wouldn't a 'god' raining down hit-or-miss misery be a moody, vindictive, indiscriminate tyrant rather than a God worthy of worship?"

"Well, when you put it that way..." As she began to speak, the sweet old woman noticed that God's head had sunk into his hands as he sagged into a defeated posture. She hesitantly stepped to him and laid a comforting hand on his shoulder.

After a moment, God reached up and patted her hand as he straightened himself.

"While man may be in charge on earth, this is *my* kingdom and you're going to love it here!" God was cheerful again as he opened the spectacular gates to a joyful, healthy hereafter for the woman to enter.

***

Child's Play

She had killed her six and nine-year-old children with a meat cleaver. Standing before God, Kim claimed to have no memory of the horrific acts and, when questioned further, claimed that 'voices' had told her what to do.

"So, Kim, that's kind of an either/or pair of statements; which is it?" God was trying to give the woman the benefit of the doubt but had doubts of his own as he tried to judge this heaven-or-hell situation fairly.

Kim was emotionless as she looked at the floor and mumbled her answer. "We were fighting, my husband and me. He got so mad that he drove down to sleep in the parking lot of our shop. The kids were mad that I let him leave and the three of us had another fight as he drove off. The voices told me to shut them up with the big knife. So I did."

"Your children were old enough to fight back and they put up a good one. None of that brawling brought you to your senses enough to stop and get them to a hospital or call for help while you still could?"

"I don't remember."

"OK, Kim. I know that on earth you got off with an insanity plea and managed to kill yourself in the mental facility. The people who judged you in court tried to give you the benefit of the doubt.

"I, however, don't buy it. First, I know mental illness, congenital or temporary when I see it. Secondly, I know you used your children as bargaining chips against your husband right from the beginning and that he had finally called your bluff. Most importantly, you've not once asked about your children; whether they're here, will want to see you... nothing.

"Beneath that timid exterior beats the heart of a born manipulator who sees no one's needs but her own. You can't game me, Kim. The devil is not going to be fooled either." God shoved down the screeching lever, sealing Kim's fate.

The rest of God's afternoon was soured by the encounter with Kim and he called it a day early. Since Peter had no one in the waiting room, the two men decided to take a stroll through the private gardens.

After a few quiet minutes, Pete asked God if it was that last woman who had left him in such a slump.

"You know me well, old friend. Did you look at her sheet, or were you reading romance novels, as usual?"

Peter chuckled at the idea of reading bodice-rippers before answering. "Yes, I read what we had on her, but it was pretty slim pickin's until the murders. A life that just seemed to de-rail with no warning, it looked like"

"Isn't that just the most insidious kind of evil? Nothing shows. The facade is so unremarkable as to be invisible. Look how many atrocities are followed up with comments from family and neighbors about all of the warning signs that authorities wouldn't or couldn't follow-up on. Even on earth everyone sees *that* train coming.

"Cases like this fly under the radar. Even with my ability to read the heart and soul of a person, I can't do one thing to avert the cursed trajectory of anything. And even if the husband *had* seen it coming, western civilizations have ceded their authority to do anything about the insane or evil among them. So here we are with those precious children among us way too early."

"Are you content with your decision to have seen the two children before their mother?" Peter asked.

"Absolutely. Before it was muted, their fear and anguish at the violent betrayal of that woman was heart-wrenching. The only good thing about their not surviving the attack is that they'll never remember things which would have haunted the rest of their earthly lives. Now the brutal assault and the woman who committed it will never cross their minds again. One of the few bright spots in the situation, right?"

"We have to take them when we find them, that's for sure." Just then, as they crossed into a more public part of the garden, Peter pointed ahead. "Look! Now, *there's* a bright spot for you!"

Kim's two carefree children were romping with their puppy who had died only months before them. Glowing great-grandparents and others were beaming in joy at the sight.

As the children spotted God, they ran gleefully and hugged him, babbling all the while about their puppy and all the fun they were having. Peter and God smiled at each other over the precious heads and gave their first real smiles all afternoon. It was a good day, after all.

***

Reincarnation

"**P**lease, please tell me I don't have to go back." The woman's voice had a pleading tone and her face matched it. Her anxiety radiated around the room.

"Back? ... Back to earth, you mean? Here, before we get further into this, Bobbie, let's have a seat, we have all the time in the world." God ushered heaven's new arrival to a pair of comfortable chairs in front of a crackling fire.

After a couple of moments while they settled into the calm, God spoke: "Now, then, Bobbie, arriving here is usually a joyous occasion for my children and I want it to be your experience, too. Tell me your concerns."

Inhaling deeply, Bobbie looked tentatively at God. "I'm sorry. I'm not much of a whiner as a rule, and I apologize for having started our conversation that way." Seeming somewhat less agitated, Bobbie began. "I was raised and lived through my young adult years among kind of a crackpot bunch of people. Oh, we all got out in the real world, had jobs and didn't really stick out, but we were different.

"The thing that's relevant to your question and my dread is that we were taught that we were going to keep coming back to earth, keep being reincarnated over and over again, until we got it right.

"Now, logically, I feel that's nonsense. But I can't help being scared witless by something I learned at such a young age. Do you understand what I'm saying?"

God breathed deeply and gave Bobbie a reassuring smile. "Absolutely. You have great communication skills, Bobbie. Your years of working with the public really show. And your life seems to have been a good one, would going back really be that bad?"

"Oh, I had a happy life. Certainly, some tragedies and sadness, but overall, I'd take my life over that of anyone I know. But once was enough. I've never been a gambler, but I suspect the odds of my going back and making as many good decisions as I did probably wouldn't be in my favor. According to the teachings of my youth, though, if you don't achieve perfection the first time around, you'll keep being sent back until you do. Just the thought of it is defeating."

"How many perfect people did you encounter on earth?" God asked gently.

"None. Zip. Zero. Nada. Or even heard third-hand of one someone *else* had known." Bobbie was anguished again and twisting the hem of her skirt. "Which is why the whole notion of there being any perfect people has never held water for me. If someone had ever proven that it could be done, maybe..."

"Let me assure you, Bobbie... it can't be done. You will run into as many or as few people here in heaven as you want to and not a single one of them was perfect. Now, children who die are perfect, but those who reach the age of making their own decisions make mistakes. Some are horrendous ones that can land a person in hell. But intention counts for a lot and, among generally decent people, remorse over bad decisions is a pretty effective learning tool.

"This place would echo like an empty bowling alley if I kept waiting for only perfect people to show up." God reached between the chairs and laid a reassuring hand on Bobbie's arm. "I promise you, my dear girl, that going back isn't an option, so please don't let the notion trouble you again."

"Seriously?! It's not even an *option?*" Bobbie's soul-deep liberation was palpable. "I feel foolish for being so relieved to hear that... whew..." Bobbie paused for a delicious moment before continuing. "After I got free of my parents' religion, I never had a church affiliation again and I'm awfully ignorant of what to expect of you or of heaven." Bobbie had begun to sound more relaxed and confident than she had a few minutes earlier.

"That's great! With few preconceived notions, it will all be a delightful surprise for you. So, do you feel better prepared for the joyful reunions waiting for you?"

As she nodded, God rose and offered Bobbie his hand, the cozy room was suffused with light as the spectacular gates materialized and a glorious day appeared beyond them. Bobbie gasped and breathed out, "Oh! There really *are* pearly gates! And its daylight...I...it was evening when we sat down. How...?" She turned to face a beaming God.

"Welcome to heaven, Bobbie! Who and whatever you hope to see will be there for you. Right now, you've got loved ones waiting to show you around, so enjoy every minute of your reward. And, my dear daughter, know you are here to stay." God held a gate open and waved the thrilled woman into the open arms awaiting her.

***

A Day in the Park

The playground was rowdy with the laughter and voices of amped-up children. Several playful dogs frolicked among them as smiling parents kept watch from benches and picnic blankets. The day was cooperating with a few clouds skittering across a blue sky.

In a shady area overlooking it all, several older folks watched in the way grandparents prefer to do; thoroughly enjoying the delightful chaos without being responsible for falls from swings.

"Oh, isn't this marvelous!" chirped Velma in her honeyed southern accent as she clapped her hands in joy. The others laughed and heartily agreed.

Her husband John put his arm around Velma's shoulders and spoke quietly: "Don't you just love looking at these kids and knowing that our twins grew up the same way?" They smiled into each other's eyes as others in the group smiled with them.

Ethel, a newcomer to this group and to heaven, looked around quizzically and said, "I feel I've turned two pages, what am I missing, if you don't mind my asking."

"Ah, well, Ethel. This is a great day for you to learn something new about heaven!" God sounded jubilant to be able to jump into a conversation that was one of his favorites. "We're all sharing the joy that Velma and John get from watching the way children grow up in heaven. Their own twins, Jimmy and Bella died at five years old in a freakish accident. Their older son wasn't involved and helped sustain Velma and John for the rest of their lives, but of course, the deaths left a void that could never be filled."

"Oh, I'm so very sorry I asked and gave you pain again...I..." Ethel stumbled over herself trying to take away the anguish she was sure she had caused.

Velma reached over to squeeze Ethel's hand and comforted, "Oh, my dear, the pain is *so* far behind us. Like you, we'd had no idea of what becomes of babies and children who die on earth. Arriving here and learning that our twins were here to greet us was the very best part of dying!"

Ethel's questioning face turned to God, who happily began to fill her in. "It's really an ingenious system, if I do say so myself; let me see if I can give you an overview. When children die on earth, they arrive healthy, just as you all do, but needing parenting. *And*, there are always young people who died before they could have or could finish raising their own children. They're content and happy here, but the chance to parent a newly arrived child who's without their own family is highly prized."

"But, isn't that a huge responsibility for a total stranger to accept?" asked Ethel. "And what if the child has grandparents, siblings or aunts and uncles already here who would like to participate? Doesn't that get ouchy?"

"Just the opposite, actually," God resumed. "The child arrives to people who love and want him for all the right reasons, who will never have to change a diaper or fear anything for the child worse than a scraped knee. The people here aren't a danger to her and we have people who are born teachers and love passing the children around to learn the world's and their families' history. There are no family jealousies, only a united effort to raise and love a kind, well-rounded person.

"Even though there are no children born in heaven, procreation being strictly man's purview, we do enjoy the young ones we have here!"

"And, best of all," John interjected, "When their birth parents do arrive, the kids know and love them! It was the most joyful reunion; no awkwardness at all, just pure, unadulterated joy. *And*, we've gained a new family in all of those who stood in for us, right?" John turned to Velma with a broad smile.

"It brings a whole new meaning to the word 'family'" Velma asserted. "Jimmy and Bella know about and enjoy children, and, although neither will have ones of their own, they are both active with babies who arrive here needing families. John and I could not be prouder of our fine young people."

"Do your twins have spouses?" Ethel asked. "I'd never have thought to wonder if people could marry or re-marry in heaven."

"Jimmy is engaged to a lovely woman, but Bella doesn't have anyone special right now."

God laughed and teased John and Velma that Bella may have a little surprise for their anniversary date coming up near Christmas.

"Christmas?" asked Ethel "Boy, I really am a dumbbell, I hadn't even thought to ask about holidays and how they're handled here. Tell me, please, I'm dying to know!"

She glanced at the others sheepishly as they snickered at her choice of words.

"Oh, we do them up royally," God enthused, "whatever your favorite, if you're interested, you'll find it here! Let's see, there's Diwali, Hanukkah, Kwanzaa, Día de los Muertos, Lohri, oh, so many all through the year and, of course Christmas with Santa. Boy, I wonder if *anyone* could name all of the holidays!"

"Probably not, if you can't," laughed John. "I was so happy to see that you allowed the children to have Christmas with Santa; it's such a rite of passage for those in our culture that Velma and I really thank you for allowing our kids to experience him. Regardless of one's beliefs on Jesus or Santa, what harm can come from allowing children the fun of celebrating giving?"

"My thoughts exactly, John." God was standing as he spoke. "Well, folks, I see that the sun is falling and everyone but us has left the park for home, shall we follow suit?" The group took it's time dispersing as they chatted and enjoyed a last moment with their friends.

It was only a few days later that John and Velma tracked God down to ask him about the broad hint he'd dropped about their daughter Bella. "Is she going to tell us that she and Chris are getting married?" John asked.

"Boy, I really blew that one, didn't I?" God sounded chagrined. "I hope you can feign surprise and bail me out. Yes, they thought your Anniversary would be a fun time to let you know they're engaged. You do like Chris, don't you?"

"Oh, very much," replied Velma, "he's probably just who we would have picked out for Bella, don't you think?" She turned to John.

"Yes, he's a great guy; I think they'll be good together." John turned to God and asked, "But what if they're not? I know there are a lot of divorced people here in heaven, but what are your thoughts on it?"

"Hoo boy, that's a sticky one! I wish every marriage was as successful as yours. You two went through times that many marriages couldn't have weathered, but not only did you stay together, you actually stayed in love. A pretty remarkable accomplishment.

"Most people keep changing as they mature and, sadly, often not in the same direction as their spouse. A twenty-five-year-old isn't usually the same person he'll be at fifty. And, at fifty, he may have another fifty years ahead of him, so it's pretty unfair to expect him to live with someone he once loved but no longer has anything in common with."

Velma smiled at John before saying, "We really made a focused effort to maintain common interests, so we didn't just drift off in opposite directions as many of our friends did. We weren't joined at the hip, but we shared a lot."

"As you saw among your friends, it takes a concerted effort. But when a marriage is really over, it's sad to stay together with no real joy left, don't you think?"

"Yes," agreed John. "It's hard on families and friends, but a divorce really can give both people a new chance at happiness if handled correctly."

"And that's a good summation of my view, too, John." God smiled ruefully as he continued. "As one who never attempted marriage, I'm always astounded at how many really do turn out well. I would never ask that a couple stay together in my name if they're miserable; even if the split doesn't occur until they arrive here; forever is too long to spend it in misery.

"You might be surprised though, at how many former or struggling couples get here and find that the smoothed edges of all heavenly transitions make them see in each other what they saw initially. Pretty sweet, sometimes. So, I would give Bella and Chris good odds on making it work!"

On that cheerful note, the three bid their fond goodbyes and set off, Velma and John hand in hand.

***

A Hole in the Universe

"*You!!*" The old woman screamed hysterically, "How *could* you?! The crazed woman came flying at God pummeling his chest as she broke into sobs before being easily subdued by God's loving arms surrounding her.

"Ada, Ada, my dear woman. Shhh. Here, let me get you a chair and a sip of water." God was guiding the distraught woman to a wooden swing with comfortable cushions. He sat next to her. "I know, I know." he soothed.

"No! No, you can't possibly know." Ada sobbed into her apron for a few moments as a deep silence settled between them.

Finally, as she tried to compose herself, Ada spoke again, "Oh, God, can you ever forgive me? I can't believe I attacked you. I'm out of my mind, but there's no excuse. Please, please forgive me."

"You were forgiven before the first blow landed, Ada. Your antenna was on high alert today for you to have known about Brighten's death in the same moment I did. I apologize to *you* for the cosmic mix-up. But since you do know..."

Ada interrupted God with a searing "What do you *mean* you knew when I did? It's your *doing*! You killed my beautiful granddaughter with that big semi-truck!"

God took his time before replying, "Ada, I know the beliefs you've held from childhood are the first ones to surface after a tragedy, but do you remember the meeting a large group of us had not too long after you got here? The one where I explained my role in life on earth?"

"I... yes... I remember your telling us that whatever happens there is by chance or by man's own hand, not of your doing. Yes, I do remember, but... you're right, my old, earthly beliefs were the ones that caused my reaction."

"It's perfectly understandable, Ada, and, it's the main reason people here aren't privy to upsetting news. This is heaven and, for the most part we don't concern ourselves with earthly matters over which we have no control. A shimmer in the ether or some freak thing caused you to know of the accident before Brighten even got here to reunite with you and all of the others. She's waiting with Peter as we speak, and you'll see her very soon."

"But what can I possibly say to that dear child? She had her whole life ahead of her. Did her baby die, too? She was eight months along with her second child. I got to hold her firstborn, you know; and it was something I'd prayed for; to live long enough to see him. He's about four by now."

"Amazingly, the baby girl did live, Ada. She is still hospitalized, of course, but her survival may make Brighten's loss a tiny bit easier for those who remain."

Ada took a long, steadying breath before asking, "And no one's responsible? It was an accident on everybody's part?"

"The truck driver was sober and doing all the right things as was Brighten. It seems that the sun may have blinded her as she rounded a curve, but anything they find will not change the outcome.

"Now, Ada, I'm going to ask you to do something for me, and, more importantly, for Brighten. Do you remember when you arrived here in heaven? You were joyful and excited about reconnecting with your family and friends, right?"

Ada gave a radiant smile, "Joyful is the right word; I don't remember ever before having such a feeling of contentment and peace. All my earthly worries had just evaporated...

"...and you're going to ask me to help Brighten to have that same experience, aren't you? To not let my own..." Ada looked momentarily confused before, with a calm sense of clarity, she smiled at God and asked him "So, you'll be bringing my granddaughter, Brighten, to me? Shall I wait here? I'm so excited; *many* people will be! Thank you for letting me be the first!"

"Ah, Ada, you are a delight." If it hadn't been ludicrous, God would have thanked God for Ada's shift back to heaven standard time. "Thank you for agreeing to be Brighten's first contact and her guide to the family. You'll all have a delightful reunion. Now, I won't keep her waiting any longer, and you enjoy this glorious day until she gets here to you." God arose and patted Ada's shoulder as he passed into the bright light awaiting him.

He felt like he'd been dragged through a keyhole.

For the most part, the universes operate smoothly, but every once in a while, there's a wrinkle in time that allows some earthly matter to pop through to heaven and it's rarely a good thing.

Taking a deep breath and smoothing his hair a bit, God slipped into his main parlor and buzzed Peter to bring Brighten in.

"Oh, Saint Peter is such a lovely man!" Brighten greeted God. "And you look exactly as I've always envisioned; I'm so thrilled to be here!"

"And we're thrilled to have you, Brighten. You must be quite a charmer yourself to have Peter behaving properly, he tends to be a little testy with most folks."

The two shared a small laugh before God cautiously ventured, "Your death was a tragic one, Brighten, but you seem to have arrived here in perfect peace. Do you have any questions for me?"

After a long pause, Brighten gently cupped her empty stomach and asked; "Why do I feel so hollow? As though I've turned twenty rather than just two pages?

"My baby! Oh, dear God, my baby girl!" Brighten whirled in a frantic circle before God got his arms gently around her and held her. He calmed her as only he could before explaining that the baby was alive and healthy. That her existence and that of her brother would be the glue that bonded the family as they healed.

"Ah, my child. Your transition to heaven was an abrupt one and you left a young family to mourn you. As you acclimate to heaven, you will have threads of your love for them begin to form a warm, loving blanket around your soul. For now, just know that you are loved by many here and on earth and you are where you belong."

The young woman considered for a few moments before replying "I'm pleased to find heaven so calming, which is all I could ever have asked of it. Am I right in guessing that my Grandma Ada will be waiting for me?"

"You are, indeed, Brighten! Your Grandma is waiting to escort you to a reunion with some of your family and I believe that your dear old dog, Shep is at the head of the line, he was a favorite, wasn't he?"

"This just gets better and better!" The young woman enthused.

God was satisfied that the time-warp hadn't affected Brighten and asked if she was ready.

"Yes, please!" she responded as she took God's arm to be escorted through the big pearlies and into the garden to meet her grandmother.

***

Third Commandment
You Shall Not Take God's Name in Vain

It was one of the group's rare daytime poker dates. Somehow, cards and a drink seemed evening activities, but here they were in the large, pagoda-styled gazebo surrounded by acres of heaven's spectacular blooming cherry trees.

Ruby had dealt and God was about to draw when Carl suddenly lurched across the table sending everything on it flying. "Goddamnitalltohell!" he shrieked, slapping frantically at the back of his neck. Fausto and God had grabbed for Ruby as her chair lurched backwards. Cards on the ground were trampled and broken glass was everywhere.

After a few minutes, it was ascertained that no one was more than shaken up and everyone quietly began to stack the sodden and broken mess on the sideboard. While he was there, Fausto raised a decanter and got a solid thumbs-up from everyone.

Finally settled in dry chairs across from the messy scene, it fell to God to ask, "Carl? Are you ok? What happened?"

Carl blew out a breath making his lips flutter. "I just don't even *know* how to apologize to all of you," he began, "I *did* swear on earth and that just slipped out because I was so terrified. It's a sorry excuse, I know, but..." he looked directly at God. "Can you ever forgive me?" he asked with eyes pleading.

"For swearing? Were you thinking about me when you said it? You appeared to have other things on your mind. Tell us what was going on."

"Talk about a couple of knee-jerk reactions," Carl began, "On earth, a bee sting would have killed me; I was beyond allergic. When I first got here today and saw all of the blossoms, the thought went through my head: 'nanner-nanner, I'm safe from you bees now!' Later, as I concentrated on my hand, I thought I felt a sting on my neck and the rest was just pure instinct. I'm sorrier than I can say; not only for making such a mess and scaring the socks off of you all, but for having taken your name in vain." Again, he looked imploringly at God.

"It was a most effective way to bring up the Third Commandment conversation!" Fausto was obviously trying to bridge a potentially awkward moment.

God stepped into the breach: "Aw, you guys. There are a lot of perfectly legitimate reasons to not swear; it makes you look coarse and uneducated, makes some of your audience uncomfortable; you know, all the things your mothers told you. But sometimes, there's just nothing that expresses your anger, fear or frustration as satisfyingly. I'd be a pretty unreasonable Father to you all if I allowed myself to judge you too harshly for it. Your fellow man might, but, for me, it's pretty small potatoes in the over-crowded 'sinning' category."

"Yes," Ruby mused, "until I got here, I never considered the magnitude of sinning you have to deal with. Though I didn't realize it until middle age, even the most horrendous crimes reported by the newspaper or TV were highly sanitized for public consumption. I guess most of the 'sins' we're cautioned against were deemed as such long before the days of social media. Now, if something truly horrendous happens, it's around the world with its most salacious details before you can blink an eye."

God rumpled his hair for a moment before answering. "You're right, most offenses are basically the same as they ever were, but there's sure no keeping a lid on the news of them these days. I fear it's made man awfully callous to the hideousness of true sins when the picayune ones are slathered across the internet for all to see.

"But maybe the upside to it is that we might gain a better perspective on what true sin looks like and what is really a piddly little offense.

"And, Carl, *yours* falls squarely into the 'piddly offense' category!"

Everyone had a good laugh and finished tidying up before setting out into a glorious sunset highlighting the glowing cherry trees.

***

The Salesman

God was in a foul mood. Why, he wondered, do they come in batches? Was this really all *my* doing?! I guess it seemed like a plan at the time, but it makes me feel like a blockhead when I look at absolute *groups* of miscreants who slipped through the cracks. People *I* created!

For some of those who show up on God's threshold for a thumbs-up or down, there's no question at all; they're going straight to hell. The only reason they even got the glimpse of God's face or heaven was to impress upon them that, no, it wasn't a mistake that they ended up as Beelzebub's flunkies. Slamming down the lever on the trapdoor gave God no pleasure; it was like balancing a checkbook, it had to be done but was no one's idea of a good time.

Now, this next guy up could go either way. Maybe purgatory wasn't such a bad idea after all. God had been tossing around the idea of eliminating it in favor of a simple yes or no decision. Best to not be hasty, he'd decided.

"Ok," God buzzed Saint Peter; "send him in."

A salesman is always a salesman. Some are great people doing their fellow man a service and then there are snake-oil peddlers and, usually, they're born, not made. Male or female, they show up in God's atelier with shoulders back, hand outstretched and smiling from ear to ear. Bert Angram was no exception. He must be good, God mused to himself; usually, by the time they get past Pete, most are a little more subdued.

The awkward silence that ensued as Bert realized his hand wasn't going to be acknowledged was brief; this was a guy who knew how to finesse. Bert took control by effusively thanking God for having made the whole dying thing so painless; "Another minute and I could have been maimed by that semi," he enthused, "It was a perfect time to have that last heart attack and go off the road!"

When God could get a word in, he mentioned that the only thing that had kept the tractor-trailer from mangling Bert was that the driver had her two kids with her that day and was momentarily slowing the rig.

"Well, whatever, it worked out!" boomed Bert.

Tiring of the chit-chat, God took control and asked Bert why he had built and served on the board of the world-famous children's hospital.

"I had the money and it looks good on my resume, right?" Bert joshed.

Ignoring the question, God asked Bert just exactly how many pyramid schemes he'd juggled to *make* all that money.

"Ah, you know about that, huh? And, judging by the yellow pad on your lap, I guess it's a rhetorical question you already have the answer to, right?"

God just stared at him, so Bert took the hint and had the good sense to look abashed. "OK, over the years they added up to five or ten. As I got better at it, they brought in more money and I was able to back off quantity in favor of quality, if you get my drift."

God rose and began haranguing Bert over the hundreds of people whose lifesavings and entire retirement funding had been wiped out during his career of crime. He told stories of those who had committed suicide or died of heart attacks caused by the ruination of their and their families' lives; all because they had trusted Bert.

"And you think that your having started a charitable foundation, (with your name plastered all over everything, by the way) makes you even?" God roared.

"I was a good tipper after I got rich; I tried to find ways to..."

"Salve your conscience? Grease the skids into heaven?" God was tired and angry. "Push that button on the wall." He waved off the sputtering questions that tried to escape the salesman's quivering mouth. "Get in the elevator and follow the instructions." God turned and walked away.

This is probably why purgatory (the only choice on the elevator's keypad) had sounded like a good idea in the first place. It gives everyone a cooling off period and the offender the opportunity to clean up his record if he's so inclined. Not all were. Some arrived there with an attitude and never learned to appreciate how fortunate they were to have not heard the squeal of the lever rather than the hum of the elevator.

Not too long afterward, God looked over the day's appointment list and saw a name that made him breathe deeply. So... another go-round with Bert Angram. The good news in a second interview with one of his children who has done time in purgatory was that they'd actually made the effort to atone for their evil deeds. Of course, God *could* overrule the committee, but it rarely happened.

The harder news was that God had to let go of his previous judgement and give the person an unbiased second look. He always made sure, in his own mind, to give his child every advantage.

Later in the day, when Peter buzzed Angram in, God approached Bert with his arms out, embraced and welcomed him with warmth. He suggested that they take seats out in the tranquil garden.

After settling in, God began, "How are you, Bert? Tell me about yourself."

"Phew. Well, I imagine you've gotten progress reports, so I'll try to be brief..."

"Actually," God interrupted, "the only report I have is that you're here. Your journey through purgatory is out of my hands until someone decides that you've made a decent transition and deserve a second shot at heaven. So let me hear your thoughts."

"'Someone,' huh? So, all of the people I'd hurt on earth and who spoke with me in purgatory are the ones who gave me the thumbs up?"

"Well, maybe not all of them. But yes, the majority of them felt that you heard and sympathized sufficiently with their stories to pitch in and save you from hell. They weren't perfect people either, you know. They know what it is to sin and be forgiven, so they're the ideal ones to gauge the sincerity of your repentance. Does that make sense?"

"Yes," Bert answered, "It really does.

"At first, it was hard to not be defensive as they began approaching me with their stories, but it took almost no time before I was in tears with the shame of what I'd done to their lives; what I'd taken from them. I've never felt that level of mortification... it's indescribable. To be faced with such a prodigious pile-up of death and destruction and to know there was no one to blame but me..." Bert was sobbing.

God quietly waited for Bert to compose himself before saying, "I'm sure it was a humbling experience... Now, try to imagine those who never make it to where you are today. Those who, when confronted by the ones they've wronged in heinous ways, basically shrug their shoulders or try to justify their actions by redirecting blame back onto their victims. The people who refuse to accept responsibility and repent for their actions are given every chance, but many don't take advantage and are sent from the relative comfort of purgatory to hell. Can you fathom that?"

A long silence before Bert whispered, "Not in my wildest dreams. If every miscreant's victims are as eloquent as mine were, it's hard to envision what kind of soul wouldn't grovel and beg forgiveness."

"Well, we certainly agree on that.

"Bert, I'm overjoyed to be able to welcome you to heaven. I forgive your sins. You are now on an equal footing with the rest of my children here.

"Neither you nor your victims will have memories of your interactions in purgatory nor of the negative ones on earth. The hatchet has been buried, so to speak. Heaven is a joyous, interactive place with no room for grudges. The moment you leave this garden, you will be as free of your sins as everyone here is of theirs."

"There aren't words enough for my thanks. I am humbled by your forgiveness..." Bert began and was interrupted by God.

"No, son, the time for that is past, this is the time for rejoicing! Now, come with me; today is your first day and you are going to love it here!"

***

The Activity Director

"You're doing *what* this afternoon?!" Gray couldn't believe that he'd heard God correctly. The two had struck up a conversation while grabbing early morning coffees from a kiosk. "You're God, for the luvvapete! And this is heaven. Why would you be doing *trail maintenance?*"

God laughed at Gray's astonishment. "Yes, it probably does sound pretty odd to someone who hasn't been here long. But, believe it or not, the day may come when you get bored with lying on the beach. When you wonder if it isn't time for planting some spring flowers or tidying the garden shed for fall. You were a gardener, as I recall?"

"Well, yes, but I guess I just assumed that all of heaven was as idyllically maintenance-free as I've experienced it. I haven't seen a blade of grass or anything else that seemed to require any attention at all."

"And, until you're ready for some busyness, you won't. People who have always enjoyed gardening love the physical activity of it as much as they do the bountiful outcome. People who were cabinetmakers crave the creativity and precision of it as much as the finished product. And people who were avid hikers often belonged to groups who participated in keeping the trails in good order.

"So, that's where I'm headed today. I'm meeting some people and repairing a few of the footbridges along one of our favorite trails. You're more than welcome to join us, Gray, you'd meet some really nice folks."

"It's tempting; sounds like a nice afternoon. But I don't have...I don't know...what about work clothes and tools, that sort of thing?" Gray paused before laughing at himself, "Golly, everything just sort of appears when you need it, doesn't it? Can't believe I never wondered where the lounge on the beach came from. Or the towel, or the margarita...wow. It's really amazing, isn't it?"

Again, God laughed. "I'm happy you think so! For the most part, things do run pretty smoothly here. Of course, if the group didn't repair those bridges, they'd never deteriorate badly enough to harm anyone, just enough to provide a nice diversion when people are in the mood. Everyone likes to feel useful, that they're contributing. And some feel more secure in having a few things on a 'schedule;' everybody's different."

"But, *you*. Aren't you the busiest person here? Why would you be repairing bridges or adhering to recreation schedules?"

God ran a hand over his hair before answering. "Doing things like working on those rustic bridges and gardening are delightful ways for me to interact with my children; to really get to know them. And to experience some of their earthly activities. I'm in a regularly scheduled poker foursome; I think the three of them value the little bit of structure in their lives and I know that all of them belong to a few other groups. For me, it's just a delight to share activities and relationships I've not experienced before.

"Do you remember a few years ago when your mother was in the hospital, Gray?"

"Of course. It was one of the most stressful times of my life, why do you ask?"

"You found comfort in your gardening and you chatted with me as you worked, didn't you?"

"Wow. *Really?!*" Gray was astounded at this very personal connection. "In the first place, I can't believe that was real...that you heard me. And how on earth could you remember such a detail?...Wait...when I first met you here in heaven, you explained, in some other context, about how the soul is our guide and solace if we'll listen to it, right? Is that what was happening?"

"Absolutely! And some of the hikers you'll meet today had similar conversations as they hiked the trails on earth. It's a genuine treat for me to nurture these connections and to be such a part of all of your lives." God sounded jubilant. "So, you're going to come along and get dirty in a little different way?"

"You bet; I'm really looking forward to it." Gray and God set off for a day of new friends and satisfying activity.

***

The Unbeliever

"**B**oy, you really *are* the atheist in the foxhole, aren't you?" God had just welcomed Bill into his private reception area with a chuckle.

"Uh, well, I guess... I mean, it was a friggin' desert without a foxhole in sight, but, yeah, I get the analogy. But if you're really God, then you know I don't believe in you, so why am I here and not in hell?"

"Is that what you've aspired to?" God asked the young Army Sergeant.

"I guess I've always avoided looking at it in such black and white terms, but probably what I would have expected if not actually *aspired* to."

"It looks like your family kind of gave lip-service to me and to religion in general and never actually insisted that you participate, is that right?"

Bill took a moment to answer... "You know, I guess that's really the way it was. Funny, I think of my mom as being a religious woman; you know, we did Christmas and Easter, but maybe those were more for the entertainment value than about you."

"And, as you got older?"

"Phew. Well, I just never thought about it. I'm sorry to have to say that to you, since I was obviously wrong, and you do exist. Really blew it, didn't I?

"I guess the turning point was when I almost married Rita...I loved her like crazy. But she and her whole family were such a bunch of whack-jobs over religion; I'm sorry, but they were over the top. It really soured the deal for me; I'd been ambivalent... agnostic, is it? But I became a full-on atheist after that. And I think I died that way, is that right?"

"Yes. The blast was so sudden and devastating that you couldn't have offered up even the tiniest prayer if you'd wanted to."

"I don't think I even know one." Bill said sheepishly.

"How do you feel about me now that I'm real to you?"

Pausing to gather his thoughts, Bill took a while to answer.

"I... I'm awestruck. I feel like my whole world is upside-down and I'm not quite sure where I fit into it."

"Actually, Bill, you're a lot less confused than most believers. You had no expectations or preconceptions. I'm a blank slate to you. The vast majority of churchgoers who arrive here are still bewildered by lifelong beliefs that didn't gel and, once they get here, they need to work their way through the contradictions. You! You're cake!"

Bill laughed out loud at God's joviality.

"Seriously, though," God continued "regardless of your atheism, you had a very strong moral direction. As I've looked through your life, I see that, with few exceptions, you tried to do the right thing. Even in breaking up with Rita, you made it about you rather than disparaging the religious fervor she and her family lived with. You were firm about it, didn't lead her on, but were a gentleman.

"What that and most all of your actions tell me is that your soul was in good working order."

"Soul?" Bill asked skeptically. "Are you telling me that souls actually exist?"

"The first and only people I created" God began, "were infused with an infinitesimal part of me. The best part, really. All of their other characteristics would change billions of times as their descendants peopled the earth, but the soul remains constant, an unbreakable connection to me, their creator. It is the single greatest source of strength and direction a person has.

"One's soul is always there, but is often unheeded. If people are bound and determined to be rotten, the soul is powerless to stop them. But, if they level out and *want* to live honorably, the soul will be there to support their efforts. There's no better compass or barometer. Does that make sense?"

"It sounds so simple." Bill mused. "It's really just trusting your instincts about what's right or wrong, isn't it? Why is it so convoluted on earth?"

"Boy, that's the sixty-four-thousand-dollar question, isn't it? The good news, though, is that life *here* is not only simple, but joyful. Bill, I know you will delight in many reunions and new friends. Welcome to heaven!" God walked Bill to the magnificent gates and the two vowed to see each other again.

It was very soon after Bill's entrance into heaven that he and God ran into each other while serving refreshments at a kid's party in the park.

"Bill! Good to see you again! What are you doing here?"

Bill laughed and responded: "That's probably an even better question for you, Sir!"

"Well, first off, I'm not Sir, just 'God' will be fine. And I enjoy grabbing opportunities to spend some time with children having a good time. But you, you were a childless young man, what's your interest in all of this; just a fan of pinatas?"

"I guess, when I heard about it, the party reminded me of my sister's five-year-old, Sari. She was a great little kid and it's fun to imagine her being part of a party like this."

Later, when the last partygoers had frolicked off and God and Bill found themselves walking from the park together, Bill wondered if he could ask a question. "Sure, what's on your mind?" God asked.

"I'm very happy here, Sir...I mean, God...I've thought so little of life on earth or anything at all upsetting, and what a gift *that* is! But, and maybe having Sari cross my mind is what did it, I suddenly wondered how my parents handled the news of my death. I mean, there probably wasn't anything left of me to send home or bury. Are they ok?"

"Sari's mom and all the others of your devastated family are helping each other to get through your loss. You will be reunited with all of them in the future. And Bill, any time thoughts like these become bothersome, you can just take a nap and await their arrival in sweet slumber."

"Thanks, I appreciate your mentioning that. But I've got more friends and family here than I would have thought, and...Oh! my dog Ranger! Thank you so much for having him here! We were in the vehicle together and I was thrilled to have him waiting here for me!"

"Ah, good, I'm happy that you and he are happy."

"One last thing if I could; having been blown to smithereens is what made me wonder I guess, but do you have any feelings one way or the other about burial
or cremation? I remember when I was a kid and one of my friends' fathers was cremated. It caused such a commotion in town that the family had to get an unlisted phone number. It's more common now, but do *you* have a preference? What are your thoughts on it?"

God paused before replying. "Bill, do you remember how instantaneous your death was?"

"It seemed shorter than the blink of a gnat's eye, thank God... you, I mean."

"And, believe it or not, that's how quickly every single soul leaves it's earthly body and arrives here. So, the 'person' on the slab at the coroner's office, dead in a car wreck, or flatlined on hospital machines is gone. The butterfly has left the cocoon on the last breath.

"The funerals and services that follow are for the benefit of the ones left behind; it's a rite of passage that those who loved him or her need. But the passage of the 'deceased' has already been made. So, whatever fits in with the emotional, religious and financial circumstances of the survivors is what they need to do for themselves... Is that an answer to your question, Bill?"

Bill laughed and replied, "Like everything here, it's perfect! So simple. Thanks for taking the time." He snagged the lone remaining balloon, handed it to God and they left the park in good humor.

***

Great Times Ahead

The two venerable women were resting with their feet up on the railing of the bustling balcony encircling the lodge. It had been a wonderful morning of skiing heaven's perfect powder. The sun and bright blue sky made it feel like an Aspen kind of day.

"Isn't God even better than you ever imagined him to be?" asked Arleen as she took a sip of hot chocolate.

Debbie laughed out loud. "Oh, boy, is that an understatement! To be able to ski again as I did when I was young, not as an arthritic old lady, just epitomizes heaven to me! When I was on my deathbed and really out of it was the first glimmer I ever got of this kind of heaven, and I don't think it was the vision that TV preacher was meaning to convey." She laughed again and asked if she'd ever told Arleen the story.

"Start it, and I promise I'll tell you if it's a re-run." Arleen smiled to her friend.

"Well, as you know, I was bed-bound for the last couple of years I lived. For the most part, my brain kept clicking, for all the good that does when you can't *do* a damned thing. The kids kept trying to get me interested in the laptop computer they'd bought me, but I could never explain to them what a foreign apparatus it was and how hard it is to learn anything new at that stage. My oldest daughter had been widowed by then and moved in to help me get through to the end; thank God I never had to go into a facility, I was so grateful to that girl!

"Since I couldn't go to church anymore, we got into the habit of listening to a famous 'televangelist' kind of guy on Sunday mornings. At first, I really liked him, he didn't yell or get dramatic, he had a sense of humor and I agreed with his viewpoint. But after a while, one of his favorite little catch phrases began to nag at me."

Debbie took a moment to ask the waiter to refresh their hot drinks. As he left, Arleen noted that all of those TV fellows had a definite habit of trying to get you to home in on certain 'punch lines.'

"You're right! That's really how it felt." Debbie confirmed. "There were several of his that he repeated on a regular basis, now that you mention it. The one that began to rattle in my head as I got weaker and more out of it was his insistence that 'there are better times ahead.'

"He never, in the years I listened to him, mentioned death. Like, if you didn't say the word, it wasn't in anybody's future. Which was okay when I didn't want to admit it either, but at some point, you have to take stock of the situation and be honest about it. I was dying and there were no 'better times' ahead for me.

"I felt cheated. Here I was with one foot in the grave and the preacher wasn't willing to bring a somber note to his broadcast and address it. So I began to interpret his 'better times ahead' schtick to mean in heaven rather than on earth. It helped a little and actually made me realize that I could get by just fine without the merry preacher.

"But by then, my daughter had come to really look forward to the Sunday preacher show. So, even though I'd have probably quit watching it, my poor baby deserved to watch it if she got something out of it. So I'd kind of cat-nap through it and catch just enough that we could discuss it afterward."

As the waiter replaced their mugs with steaming new ones, Arleen asked, "Was your daughter well? Did she get out and about?"

"She was remarkably healthy for her age, but after her retirement, she'd never developed any hobbies or anything to keep her mind occupied. I hope that, after her care-taking stint with me, she got back into the habit of going to real church and met some people."

"Do you think she knew how you came to feel about the guy on TV?"

"Yes, after I put my finger on the problem I had with him, I did tell her that I was looking forward to those 'better times' when I got to heaven. We had a nice laugh about it and I think it kind of tweaked his message for her, too."

The two friends tilted their heads back and enjoyed the perfectly safe sun on their faces.

***

The Devil in the Details

Alex was helping God to re-arrange some of the chairs and benches that had been used for an impromptu concert in one of heavens parks. Out of the clear blue sky he asked; "Is Satan your brother? A fallen angel? Or what?"

"Wow! Where did *that* come from?" God laughed. "We were discussing the guy on the fiddle; or did I miss something?"

Also laughing, Alex replied, "You're right, it *was* from left field, wasn't it? I guess the fellow's rendition of 'The Devil Went Down to Georgia' brought back something I've wondered about several times. Since arriving here in heaven I've, like most people, I guess, wondered about somebody and if they ended up in hell. Luckily, those thoughts just skitter through and don't eat at me the way they might have when I was earthbound. But hearing that song again jogged me to ask."

"There are a million theories on the devil, aren't there? And the guy has a million names; Satan, Lucifer, and Beelzebub are just a drop in the bucket! I wish I could give you a more dramatic answer, but the truth is nowhere near as spellbinding as the prodigious storytelling he's engendered. Shall we sit for a moment?" God indicated a couple of the chairs still askew.

After they got their chairs leveled out, God leaned forward with his elbows on his knees and began, "When I planned the world, I realized that there would be a certain number of miscreants whose deeds would make them unredeemable; unworthy of heaven. There needed to be a place of permanent exile, punishment and damnation for the worst of the worst. So, hell it was. And I kind of left it at that.

"Some time later, I realized that there needed to be an overseer to keep things from getting out of hand down there. At about the time I was rolling the foreman idea around, this guy from what would now be called the Middle East area showed up and was obviously going straight to hell. Beelzebub was so vile that it still offends me just to think of him. You wouldn't believe some of the debauchery he dreamed up"

"Like what? It's hard for me to *imagine* what could shock you!" Alex was open-mouthed as he asked.

"Well, this was early on and I probably wasn't as bullet-proof as I've become. And, I wasn't as much shocked as totally repelled. I couldn't even say this if there were women or children around, but you asked. The guy was an agricultural overseer of sorts in a pretty primitive area and time. When one of the workers did something that Beelzebub didn't like and he wanted to make an example of the poor wretch, he forced the worker to eat whatever human excrement was lying around. With the others watching."

The two men sat in appalled silence for a minute or two.

"Beyond disgusting, I know... When he got here, I gave him two choices: to go to hell and eat nothing but that diet *himself* for all eternity or to become a better overseer under my ownership of hell. He didn't have to think it over.

"There are certainly some gruesome, fiery scenes in hell, but there are also long stretches of killing boredom. There's no recreation or camaraderie. No gardens or sunlight, it's a dreadful place."

"And Beelzebub is still in charge of it?"

"Yes; he had to be reined in a couple of times early on, but he knows that he has me watching him, so it's worked out."

"Wow. That's an amazing story. Do those who go to hell really toil for all eternity, then?"

"Oh, not really. Except for Beelzebub himself, who's earned a few foremen and a couple of perks, everyone else is eventually just taken out of the picture. They become literally nothing and their story is finished. I want hideous people to pay for their sins, but, if the punishment went on for too long, it would hurt me more than it did them, so no, it's not for all that long."

God sounded sad and deflated.

"I'm so sorry I asked about all of this; I can see how draining it's been for you." Alex felt like a heel.

"Thanks, Alex. It *is* draining, but the upside is that it makes me so happy to see how many more of my children make it here to heaven than end up in the netherworld. Overall, the odds are amazingly on man's landing here rather than in hell.

"On that upbeat note, shall we get the rest of these chairs put back in place?"

The two men finished up and, as they turned to leave the park, Alex was treated to sharing in the holy light that greeted God.

***

A Slave to the Times

"Some of the ancestors I want to look up, now that I'm here, were slaveholders. Does that mean they went to hell and my questions will go unanswered?"

"Ah, yes," God replied, "You're the genealogist, aren't you?"

Mike had enjoyed his interview with God up until now, but he couldn't leave without asking the question that had nagged him for years. "Yes, it's been a lifesaver of a hobby for me in the last thirty years or so. But, no matter how many ship's manifests or birth certificates you dig up, it's pretty rare to feel like you have any inkling of the personalities involved.

"I've always fantasized about actually getting to know those long-ago people from my tree. Is it going to be possible?"

"Oh, yes, of course, you'll be able to meet and get to know all of the ancestors in your tree who are here," God blew out a long breath before continuing, "As to the slave owners... Mike, the world has changed and evolved from day one. You were born into a time and country where the thought of slavery was abhorrent to almost everyone. But that wasn't always the case. Part of my job is to judge people's actions on earth, that's true, but I've always made it a practice to judge by the norms and mores of person's era; the times he lived in. Does that make sense to you?"

"So, if some ancient Egyptian slaveholder arrived here in 2400 BC, you didn't flash forward to today's ethics when you decided his fate?" Mike was pondering all of the implications.

"Right. And, of course, there are many other factors in every slave-owner's life; they were much more dimensional than that. Every era has had its own societal conventions and those were the guidelines people should have been trying to adhere to."

Mike raised his eyebrows. "So, how people treated their slaves really only counts if they were in or outside the prevailing norm?"

"Pretty much." God was finding this to be an interesting exercise. "Of course, any person in any timeframe was honest or not, traded fairly with his neighbors or cheated them; had families he neglected or honored. Monstrous cruelty to anyone, slave or not, is usually a deal-breaker; it takes a lot to offset that. Those factors and others figure mightily into the up or down decision.

"Looking at your chart of the few generations you're aware of, I see only one guy who didn't make the cut and that had to do with transgressions unrelated to his ownership of slaves. I imagine that your third-great-grandfather will be able to fill you in on his brother's sorry history."

"Wow! Just to hear you speak so casually about old Heinrich Bakker is unbelievably exciting!" Mike was bouncing with enthusiasm.

"Before you meet these folks, you should know you'll also probably encounter some of their former slaves. I don't want to temper your enthusiasm, but do want you to know that everyone's on a level playing field, here. Respect and courtesy are of paramount importance in your interactions. You're a generally nice guy and I don't foresee any issues, but just wanted to mention it.

"Mike, one other thing I don't think you're aware of is that you do have some mixed-race relatives. It's pretty rare for these family members to show up in genealogy searches not coordinated for the specific purpose of uniting descendants of slave owners and their 'illegitimate' relatives. While the circumstances of the birth of their great or great-great-grandparents has usually been tempered by the time people get here, it can lead to some delicate conversations."

"Wow. I appreciate the heads-up on that. No, I've never seen any such suggestion in any of the documentation I've found... but I guess it makes sense, doesn't it, that it would be covered up on the side of the slave-owner?"

"Yes," replied God, "and, of course, the slaves themselves were often kept illiterate and had no documentation to pass down even if they wanted to. A lot of what has been cobbled together now that the internet can get unlikely people together, is from family histories that were passed down orally until some descendant did actually put them in writing.

"Are you okay with all this, Mike? Is a lot for you to absorb?"

"Actually, I'm even more excited than I first was. I imagine that anyone who finds slave owners in his tree has the trickle of doubt go through about whether their ancestors may have sired children with their slaves. But, it's such a daunting prospect, the search, I mean, not the possible results, that I sure didn't follow up on it. And here, you've done all the hard work!"

God laughed aloud as he rose to usher Mike out. "Well, I'm so happy to hear your enthusiasm! I hope to run into you before long and hear of your adventures."

Through the following months, Mike had a great time catching up with most of the family and friends he'd known on earth. It was gratifying, if not too surprising that there weren't any conspicuous absences.

One of the ones Mike ended up spending a lot of time with was his Aunt Lottie. Lottie had been one of his earliest influencers in genealogy. Even when he was very small, Mike had been fascinated by his aunt's collections of family memorabilia.

In the shelves at one end of her living room, Lottie had albums full of old tintypes of relatives much older than she was, a couple of fragile old christening gowns, some leather button-up baby shoes and so much more. It was all meticulously cataloged and endlessly intriguing to the small boy.

When Lottie died, her daughter Gilda, Mike's cousin, inherited most of the treasure trove of family history. The cousins had always been close and their shared interest in the family's genealogy was intensified when the internet made research so much easier.

Gilda was still on earth, but Mike had made a beeline for Lottie. She had made many new discoveries she was eager to share with him. Yes, she assured him, there were more generations of people here that his wildest dreams would have hinted. And yes, there were still connections waiting to be made; they teamed up and had a great adventure every time they got together.

As it turned out, there were only three children who had been sired by the slaveholders in the family, but as those kids' families continued to grow down through the generations, it added up to quite a large contingent not even counting those still on earth.

Some of the 'illegitimate' family members had been, while on earth, pretty hostile toward any attempts at 'family reconciliation' but as with everything else in heaven, it was easier here. Anger and resentment had softened into curiosity. So, while Mike's extended family may never have the ties that bind the individual clans together, maybe they will.

***

Fourth Commandment
Remember the Sabbath Day

Carl shuffled like the card-shark he'd always fancied himself. With flashy arches and fans, it was quite the show and everyone always oohed and aahed when his turn came around. The four poker hands were dealt almost before the cut was finished.

As it happened, Carl's shuffling had been the best part of an unremarkable game; and everyone was glad to fold 'em on this night.

Fausto was the first to speak up as the gaming area was tidied and the visiting got underway. "It's been a few months since we had one of our 'Ten Commandments' discussions, are you up for one? I'm curious about the rationale behind the fourth... remembering the sabbath. Are we up for it?"

"Sure! It's Wednesday, so we can't get into too much trouble." After her disastrous game, Ruby was leery of more trouble.

God, the last to weigh in on this one, actually took the bull by the horns. "Well, since I'm the default expert on this ten-part discussion, I'll just put in my two-cents' worth right off the bat, how's that?" Smiling at nodding heads and a thumbs-up, God took a moment to order his thoughts.

"Again, I'll preface it by saying that they weren't *my* commandments. There's nothing inherently wrong with any of them, but this one in particular presumes a lot. The basic premise is that I finished creating the world on the sixth day and needed a rest; that rest fell on the seventh day. People do acknowledge that a 'day' in God-years can be many millennia, but there's a lot of scholarly work done attributing the creation of a seven day 'week' and the names of those days to a bunch of ancient people at least as credibly as to me.

"As for it being a day of rest, everybody certainly needs one and I don't mind being the catalyst for it. People tend to feel guilty if their noses aren't at the grindstone, so having a universally acknowledged day off is fine by me."

A long silence followed. Ice tinkled in a couple of tumblers before Carl blustered, "Well, alrighty then, that just about covers it... How 'bout those Dodgers?"

***

Settling the War of Worlds

"This could be a long visit; maybe we should all find a seat." God was speaking with a group of people in one of heaven's ellipse gardens, a more formal area than many.

The group who had waylaid God on this green, flower-filled expanse were bound and determined to get some answers.

It's the natural impulse for people of different nationalities and religions to meet and compare notes. Those interactions in heaven have much more peaceful outcomes than the interminable wars waged on earth over beliefs, boundaries and lifestyles.

Here, everyone sees the God they had loved and worshiped, in whatever manner or by whatever name. Few see the same visage when their eyes rest on God; they see *their* God. And he speaks the language they are most comfortable with; whatever languages bounce around a tableful of people, each one hears what sounds most familiar to them; a true universal language.

Everyone here also has the option of being seen as the self they're feeling like. Twenty or sixty, as an amorphous aura or in a baseball uniform. No 'bad hair days,' shaving nicks or too-tight jeans. Talk about heaven!

"So, if I understand the question correctly, you want to know why I caused the horrific cultural divisions among all of your peoples, is that right?"

"Yes." Salima, a Muslim, spoke up. "Why, on earth, were some of us made or encouraged to wear specific headgear or kurtahs that announced to the rest of the world what religion we practiced? That restricted our freedom with no apparent benefit to us?"

"Or had to have a dollop of red on our foreheads that did the same thing?" Prisha added, reflecting on her Hindu beliefs.

"As we've all talked about it," interjected Daiko, a devout Buddhist, "it seems that almost all of the Eastern women were required to cover at least their hair and, in some cases, almost everything. We men, except for the Jews, didn't usually have nearly as many constraints. We had styles, of course, but not much we were either forced or forbidden to wear."

"*But* we do have to say five prayers every day at prescribed times and places." added Laraib, a lifelong Muslim.

"Whoa..." God was trying to get a word in among the excited chatter. "Now, I know that there were myriad rituals, jewelry and head-covering requirements in your many religions and cultures, and I can see why that would cause questioning now, even if you didn't have the freedom to ask while you were on earth. I think the first question to address is: why would I command anyone, even if I could, to wear or not wear certain things? How could your clothing possibly be relevant to me? Or your hair being covered or a cross or medallion being worn at your neck?"

As God watched the slightly confused faces turn back and forth, Bisma, another Muslim woman, straightened her shoulders and asked, "What do you mean 'even if you could'? You're God. Most of us wore burqas, garments or yarmulkes precisely because you commanded us to, right?"

"Way to listen, Bisma! You got right to the heart of the matter." God's radiant smile warmed and calmed the restive group. "All of those strictures (put primarily onto women, by the way) were devised by man in the name of whatever religion he was promoting. Most religions began as a way to honor and please me, but, believe me when I tell you that I didn't hand down instructions on how to do so."

"The Ten Commandments weren't yours?" barked Ezra in his distinctive Israeli accent; "That makes no sense. They represent the foundation of life for many of us."

"And they're pretty good advice, for the most part," God began, "but they didn't come from me. This is always one of the hardest conversations I have with my children... when you ask these questions. Truthfully, I would never bring the subject up if I could avoid it. I won't lie if you ask, but it's a thorny topic."

The men and women shifted uncomfortably on their benches and chairs.

"Please don't worry," God soothed, "there's no *bad* news here, but certainly some new and freeing ways of looking at things. If you're here in heaven, valhalla, nirvana, olam habah, paradise or whatever, you've been absolved of your earthly sins. Though you have no memory of it, some of you may have made a stop in purgatory to atone for acts of real wickedness, but you're all home and equal now.

"Home is where you are safe and loved. Your strictures are few and manageable. Your religious and cultural differences on earth do not define you here. If you had traditions that gave you joy, then enjoy them here but wars will not be fought over them, shunning will not occur, and demands will not be made.

"Whether you followed the bible, the Bhagavad Gita, or any other scripture, all of those rules and laws were made by man, not me. Over some busy eons, I created the universe, man and beast then came home to heaven to prepare for your arrival. Human men and women are the stewards of earth. The climate varied and certainly influenced lives, but it was all out of my hands when the initial creation was complete. Evolution took it from there." God looked around at the confused faces surrounding him.

"You're all stunned, aren't you? I can see how unhorsed you are and I'm sorry to have upended everything you believed for your whole lives."

After a few minutes of dazed quiet, an excited chatter began. Finally, Laraib turned back to God and mused "That's why we all get along so well here, isn't it? Not only have we not branded ourselves but we're not fighting over religion. We actually know God. We know you as a real being, not as whatever some zealot has made up."

"Yes," interjected Ruth "you're real and have provided us with a wonderful hereafter! I love that we can argue over whether Sam fudged on Hanukards, but it's all going to dissipate before there's any real anger."

"This turned out to be a much more uplifting discussion than the one I was prepared for." Faiz rumbled in his deep voice, " I was sort of afraid that we were going to rip off a bandage and find something ugly."

Again, the happy babble began and, as it did, God rose from his chair. "Thanks to all of you for making me so very proud of you. Always, but today in particular. This has been a great family gathering!" He began patting backs and shoulders as he wove his way into the brilliant light that usually awaited him.

***

The Shopping Cart

The old couple huddled together next to their beat-up grocery cart behind an abandoned building. They always tried to sleep in shifts to give some protection to their belongings. Ed's wheezing had gotten steadily worse as the weather had gotten colder, but he was trying to stay awake while keeping one arm over Susan's shoulders.

The two homeless, decrepit old folks looked harmless to passersby, but you don't live on the streets for thirty years or more without having a tough hide. Either Ed or Susan could pick your pocket or kick your ass in a New York minute. Each of them had a mildly unsavory history, but neither had served time for much other than the occasional vagrancy charge back in the day when that was still a chargeable offense. For the most part they were their own worst enemies.

As Ed's sleepy head began to nod toward Susan's, he heard a voice that jerked him awake. "Get back!" he croaked out as he struggled to stand. Susan flopped to the side and began, through the constant pain, to get herself upright, too.

"Get outta here!" Ed persisted as he tried to focus on where the voice had come from.

"I'm just asking what on earth keeps the two of you going?" came a distinctly non-threatening but still disembodied voice.

"Let me see you, you cowardly sonofabitch," snarled Susan.

"Well, OK, but brace yourselves. I don't want to look like a street person or you're likely to attack me," God intoned as he began to materialize there in the alley.

After a long silence, Ed muttered: "Well, you look like I've envisioned God, but what would you want with either of *us*?"

"Please, just tell me what it is that keeps you going? You're living a life that most people would kill to get out of, yet every day you wake up and do it all again. Your days must each feel like a week long."

"All of that." Susan's voice had softened. "Are you here to give us directions to hell?"

"Is that what you're expecting? Is that why you don't surrender to death?"

"Well sure. Though I don't guess we've ever made a pact or anything. Or even talked too much about it. Have we?" Ed turned to Susan.

"Not directly, no. It's been more of an understanding, I guess. We both feel pretty sure that hell is what we've earned and don't want to get there any sooner than we have to."

"You both grew up in horrible homes and always accepted this kind of life as your fate rather than striving to rise up," God said. "Why do you suppose some people live through terrible childhoods yet go on to better their station in life?"

"I don't know, and I've wondered." answered Ed and waited expectantly.

Susan broke the long silence. "Maybe some of us had just used it all up by the time we came of age. I felt like an old, defeated woman by the time I was eighteen. Except for anger, I don't think I ever had a spark of energy or hope again in my whole life."

"That might be better than feeling hope and having it tossed back in your face at every turn." added Ed. "Sometimes, I thought... oh, well, hell, nothing ever came of any of it and I guess my determination was pretty short-lived."

The old folks sagged into each other and slid back down the wall into a sad heap.

"I'll let you two get on back to sleep." As he melded back into their souls, God reached out and caressed their heads gently. "Hold tight to each other, don't worry about the stuff in the cart and know that hell isn't your destiny. Sweet dreams."

Morning dawned to find the dazed couple waiting in heaven's vestibule. Peter informed them that they would meet with God individually but be reunited afterward. After a few moments, he looked back at them, gestured, and intoned, "It appears to be Ladies Day, Susan; please enter the opening door."

On crossing the threshold of the light-filled room, Susan was greeted by God walking toward her with his hands out.

"Holy smoke! It's you! I... I saw you before, didn't I? You're *really* God and I'm really in heaven?"

"Welcome, Susan. You actually felt me as much as saw me, and you saw me as you'd envisioned me. And I'm glad you're here. Please, have a seat." God motioned toward a pair of comfortable upholstered chairs. "You look very well rested and ready for a new adventure; how do you feel?"

"Grateful." Susan answered. "Confused, but grateful. With my life..."

God interrupted, "Shh, dear. Don't try to remember the past right now; your life obviously wasn't as shameful as you imagined or you wouldn't be here, would you? You will have many joyous experiences and I want you to enter heaven with your heart open to them."

After a few more minutes of comfortable chit-chat, God rose and helped her from her chair, "Now, I'm going to ask you to wait in the garden just beyond the gates...." He was interrupted as Susan spoke in awe "Oh! Oh, the gates! They really are made of pearls! They're glorious!" God relished her joy for a moment before they moved forward. "Susan, enjoy the peace and beauty here and Ed will join you soon. We'll see each other from time to time; be happy, my child."

On cue, Ed entered the room and laughed out loud. "I'd recognize you anywhere!" he gazed fondly at God.

"I'm glad to have you here, Ed. You'll find peace and comfort in heaven; and all the activities you ever dreamed of.

"You'll also find," God paused delicately, "Marti." At Ed's sharp intake of breath, God resumed, "Now, Marti went on to make a good life for herself after you left, and the odds of you running into each other are probably remote, but I thought that, if you and Susan are going to stay friends, you might want to let her in on your little secret. Things like this usually get smoothed over in the transition, but you never know."

"Okay, yeah, I appreciate it. Jeez, man, do you go through this kind of stuff all day, every day?"

God laughed and explained that the term 'day' is very elastic here, but yes, he stays busy. "Now, Ed, Susan is waiting for you just beyond the gates, and I know the two of you will find more loved ones waiting for you than you're expecting. Go and enjoy your reward." God gripped Ed's shoulder as he held the gate for him.

***

History in the Making

"**B**ut, with a little notice, I could've come up with some real *questions* for the man." Charles and a few others were agog over the historic figure who had just stopped by their outdoor table to say 'hi' to God before continuing on with his walk.

"Right?" replied Karen, "I was so tongue-tied at seeing Julius Caesar stroll by that I couldn't have initiated a conversation if I'd wanted to! History was my major in college and, I swear, not one thing except 'omigod!' went through my thick head."

"Well, you're being a little harsh with yourself, Karen." God stepped into the conversation. "For one thing, seeing Caesar was a surprise to *all* of us, wasn't it?" He paused and glanced around at the nodding heads. "Most of my children here in heaven have a tendency to hang around with those who are most like them, in eras or families they were familiar with on earth. We all have the ability to understand and be understood linguistically by anyone, but a certain tribalism seems innate. It's great though, to see someone with the chutzpa and curiosity to go out and mingle.

"Now, here's a fun question: if *you* were to step out of your comfort zone and look up someone of historic prominence, who would it be?"

For a minute or two you could hear brains humming as everyone pondered the possibilities. Finally, Phil popped up with "For me, it would have to be George Washington, but I would never, even now that I see it might be a possibility, have the gall to intrude on his privacy. He must be number one on so many lists, it would feel like hounding him."

"Which is probably why something like the Caesar sighting is so rare," God smiled. "It's just people's nature to stay with the 'safe zones' we all have. What about you, our history major, into whose era would you ramble?"

Karen hesitated, but finally spoke up, "Mine isn't very far back in time, either, but first on my list would be Marie Curie. Her story was one of the first that resonated with me as being a woman in a pioneering role, as someone real, not almost mythical like Cleopatra, but as a real-world woman doing important and respected work.

"I wasn't ever what you'd call a women's libber, and was raised to believe I could do anything, so just sort of approached life with that mindset. I've always felt that Marie could relate."

"Oh, that's a good one!" Charles enthused. "Male or female, that's a hard body of work to top. I haven't ever wondered too much about how we choose our 'heroes' in life, but this discussion is going to have me giving it some thought. Until I do ponder it some more, I can't even tell you *why* the guy I'd most like to run across on a stroll through the woods is Benjamin Franklin.

"Besides his obvious brilliance in myriad fields, Franklin has always struck me as a genuine, multi-dimensional person. He had faults that neither he nor his biographers seemed compelled to gloss over." Charles laughed and continued "I always, even as I got older, thought that I'd love to own and operate a bar-coffeehouse sort of place that would serve as a gathering spot for people who loved to discuss the topics of the day. Kind of a salon like the Bloomsbury group would participate in. I'd have called it 'Junto' after Franklin's group of like-minded thinkers of his day.

"I had a good life and one with few regrets; but that's one of them, not having made that dream come to fruition."

God smiled and encouraged; "Well, Charles, there's no time like the present! And running a business here is a dream compared to earth; no OSHA regulations or IRS."

"Are you kidding me?!" Charles was dumbfounded that such a venture was even possible here in heaven. "There're privately-owned *businesses* here? Why would anyone let themselves in for the headaches? Why haven't I ever seen one?"

'Oh, you see them every day, you're sitting in one as we speak! But business models here are different than you're used to. *Nobody* here needs money, services or products, so the people who feel the need for, say a cafe, just run it by me and if it sounds like something that would be popular, I'll give it the go-ahead. You know that place that serves the fabulous Honey Walnut Prawns? A fellow started it probably a hundred years ago and when he decided to take a nap, a woman took it over and it just keeps going. No supplier hassles, staffing issues, or even dirty dishes if you don't want them. Here, you get all the fun, busyness and camaraderie of a coffee kiosk, but no skirmishes with the health department or spoiled food in your cafe. It would be the same with your salon; if people enjoy what you create, it will be a joy to *you,* too. This is heaven!"

Phil had picked up on the excitement and turned to Charles, " Maybe you could even get ol' Ben Franklin as a partner! Just think of all the people he knows who would stop by! You could..."

"Whoa!" God laughed, "Your enthusiasm is great and I'm not going to throw cold water on any of it, but do consider, Charles, that, if you offer to serve people, you are making a commitment; it needs to be something you truly love and have an aptitude for, okay? Some businesses do fall out of favor due to changing tastes, but we try to keep the turnovers to a minimum. Failure and annoyance are not heavenly feelings, so I like to avoid them."

"Oh, but doesn't this sound like a terrific opportunity for Charles to fulfill a dream?" Karen asked as she looked around the table.

Karen, Phil and God were laughing and chattering excitedly, but Charles sat there with a dreamy, faraway look on his face. Who would have thought heaven could get even better?

A few weeks, months or years later, Charles was puttering around in the space that was becoming his club. He'd been very disciplined in forcing himself to go slowly. On earth, he'd seen among family and friends the pitfalls of diving into something headlong and had learned at a young age to 'measure twice, cut once' as the saying went. He'd already designed a massive wood burning fireplace in his head before realizing that it was possible to have more than one of them. What freedom! He wanted the rooms to be collegial and welcoming, not grand and cold, so it was a bit of a juggle. As he considered placement for one of the paintings, he heard the door open.

Turning, he saw a young man walking in and looking around. "Hi, can I help you?" Charles greeted him "As you can see, we're not open for business yet..."

"We. Have you taken a partner?" Asked the newcomer.

"Uh, no... I'm sorry," Charles began thoughtfully, "do I know you? Can I help you with something?"

The stranger's right hand came shooting out as he laughed, "I apologize! I was so fascinated by you and your place; I've been very rude. Ben Franklin, here." At Charles' astounded face, Franklin smiled; "You were expecting the long white hair and spectacles, I imagine?"

When Charles finally found his voice and got his hand out for the shake he sputtered, "Mr. Franklin! What an honor to meet you! And I... no, I wasn't 'expecting' anything... not you or anything *about* your looks. What... how on earth... how did you hear about Junto?"

"Well, I believe I had a little something to do with the naming of it, isn't that right?" Ben teased with a cocked head and a crafty smile.

The two men immediately fell into a discussion about the original Junto or Leather Apron Club, as it was also known. When Charles asked why Mr. Franklin hadn't ever opened a Junto Redux here in heaven, Franklin replied, "First, it's Ben, *please*! I've only just waked from a long nap and the first scuttlebutt I heard was about your venture, so I had to come and check it out. It will be so much more interesting *now*, won't it? I've rested for a couple of centuries and just think how many brilliant people of different eras we could attract now!"

Charles had heard of heaven's marathon naps but had never knowingly spoken with someone who had slept for over 200 years. "Wow," he laughed, "no wonder you look so young and chipper! And you said *WE*...really? Would you honestly consider being a part of this?"

"I'd be honored if you would allow my participation. I love the atmosphere you've created here, Charles; it feels so intimate and homey, every chair and sofa begs for your behind! I'm curious, though; what inspired you to name the little library 'The Julius Caesar Room'?"

Laughing, Charles told a quick version of the genesis of Junto and asked Ben if he thought they had a snowball's chance Caesar might drop in. Ben smiled and allowed that stranger things had happened.

Before the two men could have imagined, the stocked bar was tapped into and the fireplaces were stoked. Before they blinked, there were small and large groups scattered around and the muffled sounds of vibrant discussion and clinking glasses were everywhere. Tables of chess players, a pianist in the corner and, in every nook and cranny, excited, stimulating conversations hummed. Charles had a partner in his new venture.

***

A Good Connection

God and Nancy had enjoyed a pleasant and welcoming interview and were about to wrap-up when God said. "Oh! I almost forgot! Nancy, a fellow who arrived here a couple of years ago asked me to give you a message."

Nancy laughed ad told God that she wouldn't have imagined him as a messenger.

Flipping the pages of his yellow pad, God chortled and responded, "It happens now and then. Most of the time, I prefer that people make their own connections once they're settled. It's very easy to do, by the way; whoever you want to contact is only a thought away and we don't have any stalkers or jerks here, so most interactions are pretty comfortable. Ah, here it is." God glanced at his notes before looking up and smiling.

"Nancy, do you remember when you were in your early twenties and worked as a telephone operator for a while?"

"Wow! Boy, that was back in the dark ages!" She laughed. "That job hadn't crossed my mind for years and years; what an amazing thing for you to bring up. But, yes, I'm surprised at what a complete picture popped into my head when you mentioned it.

"I know I'm interrupting, but can I tell you a funny snippet?" At God's smiling nod, she continued. "My best friend, then and until the day I died, and I both got jobs at that huge phone company as switchboard operators. Very soon after we were hired, she, who had hoped she could keep her pregnancy a secret for a while, began barfing all over her huge switchboard. It only took a couple of times before the management had to cut their losses by letting my friend go. I hadn't thought of it for years!"

God chuckled at the sight of Nancy's mirth as much as at the story. After a few moments he began, "There's another interaction you may remember. One mid-morning you took a call from a befuddled fellow. He first asked who you were and how the two of you had connected. You assured him you were the 'operator' he had dialed and asked how you could help him. He fumbled around and asked a garbled series of questions about the day of the week, time of day and that sort of thing. Do you have any recollection of that call?"

"Yes, as soon as you began telling of it, I did remember. I don't have a verbatim recall, but yes, everything you mentioned certainly rings a bell. What on earth could a sixty-year-old phone call matter now?"

"The man whose call you handled very professionally, but with compassion, is the one who asked me to relay his thanks to you. When he arrived here, he was a pleasant man who had lived a good life and I was happy to welcome him to heaven. Before he left this room to meet his family, is when he asked me to tell you when you got here that you saved his life.

"He was only about ten years older than you and had tried to kill himself the night before that call." At Nancy's sharp intake of breath, God paused before continuing, "When he awoke and began to realize that the pills hadn't worked, his first thought was 'Thank God I have a gun to finish the job with.' But in his stupor, the phone was the first thing his hand fell on. He pushed the 'O' and there you were. He told me that the kindness and youthful optimism in your voice somehow flipped a switch and he hung up with a whole different attitude. He credits you with saving his life. Isn't that an amazing story?"

Nancy's stunned silence lasted for at least a minute. Finally, she tried to reply. "I...I...don't even know how to respond. Certainly, I'm happy for him that he went on to a good life. But to credit it to me..." She lapsed again into silence.

Gently, God intoned, "Isn't it a wonderful illustration of the benefits of being kind to your fellow man for no reason other than being kind? Many people wouldn't have remembered that interaction with as much appreciation and awareness, but I'm so glad to be the one to share his thanks with you."

"Well, I certainly appreciate it, thank you. You're right about the illustration of the value of kindness. It's also an amazing example of the power of gratitude, isn't it? That the fellow remembered it with such appreciation for so many years! And to have had the presence of mind to mention it to you on such a momentous day as this. I'm humbled beyond words."

"I'm always so proud of my children when they display the deep goodness you and he did, Nancy. I can see why your own Daddy is waiting outside the gates with such joy; we're both proud of our daughter! Are you ready?" God stood and offered his arm for the short walk to the gates and the joy awaiting beyond them.

***

Fifth Commandment

Honor Your Father and Your Mother

The four poker players had tidied up after a satisfying game and were settled into their favorite chairs. For a change of pace, Fausto had whipped up Margaritas served in tall, stemmed glasses. The conversation was flowing.

"But, how on earth can you argue that there's an option to honoring your father and your mother," responded Carl to Ruby's comment; "they conceived and raised us, they're our whole foundation."

The topic tonight was the fifth commandment and it hadn't taken long to see that there was more than one opinion on it.

God asked: "Ruby, I feel there's more to your little 'not necessarily' quip. Do you care to share with us?"

"Well, as *you*, at least, know, I had great parents. They were all that Carl is envisioning with his comment and I do honor them for their efforts. Now. It took a while, though, to really appreciate them. I guess we all get to a certain age, probably when we have kids of our own, when we realize what smart-mouthed brats we'd been to our folks when we were younger. Forgiving that is just a part of parenting."

"Tell me about it!" cracked God. "I'm sorry, Ruby, carry on..."

"I had a friend when I was in my teens who had the world's worst parents. I've always thought that they were even worse than uneducated dopers who treat their kids badly out of ignorance. These folks were highly respected in our town and looked great on the surface. But my friend and her sister were sexually abused by their father from the time they were toddlers. The mother knew about it and told the girls a lot of variations of 'you're just imagining things, don't you dare mention such a crazy thing to another living soul.'

"Of course, it all ended badly. But neither parent was ever held to account for the lifelong damage they conspired to inflict on those kids. I wish I thought theirs was a singular story, but I know it's not." Ruby took a moment to compose herself.

"Sadly," intoned God, "you're right; I wish it wasn't so, but it is. I will tell you though, that those parents and others like them *are*, eventually, held to account. You won't run into them here in heaven.

"It's wonderful when parents are of the sort who deserve to be honored. They're all imperfect, as every human is, but the ones who make the effort to be the best parent they can be, deserve everyone's thanks. There are many levels between what Ruby described and the very best, but even flawed people can love and do their finest for children they genuinely love. Sometimes 'good enough' really is."

"So, it sounds like, as with the other commandments, there's a lot of wiggle room?" asked Fausto.

"Yes, a lot." God resumed, "Some, like Ruby's neighbors, go straight to hell, some come here, and some do a stretch in purgatory before earning heaven. Parenting is a hard job; I've often scolded myself for making pregnancy so fun and easy to accomplish!"

"For sure, a lot of people weren't cut out to be parents," Fausto began, "my sister wasn't abused in the sense that Ruby's friend was, but our mother managed to ruin their relationship, anyway."

Carl sighed, "Well I guess it was too much to hope that all three of us had good parenting. How did *you* get on with your mother?"

Fausto gave a self-deprecating laugh and said, "Oh, well, I'm a born caregiver, so I was the referee and peacemaker all rolled into one. I can see a lot of the effects of our raising in me, but they're more benign than what Sis was left with. Are you sure you want to hear this?"

Everyone agreed that it was still early and there was one more round of margaritas left in the shaker, so, yes, please.

Fausto did the shaking and pouring and began his story... "Mom was a falling down drunk who chased our dad off very early on. He and our grandparents really raised us with mom drifting in often enough to cause chaos. As you can see, I turned out perfect..." he paused for the rowdy laughter..."but Sis was always mom's target. By the time mother was old, she was all in Sis's corner, but it was kind of late by then. Sis struggled all her life with the addictions that mom had demonstrated so ably for her child, but with a better end result.

"They both died before I did and, when I got here, I was surprised to see the two of them in the same waving family reunion that greeted me. I had wondered if one or both of them had committed some dire crime that might have sent them to hell, but more, if they were even speaking to each other if they *were* both here." Fausto paused.

"But they were together to greet you?" asked Carl.

"'Together' would be a stretch." Fausto continued, "They appear to have a decent relationship based on some few good memories, but it's obviously not nearly as deep as those Sis has with our grandparents, dad and step-mom. You reap what you sow, I guess."

God reiterated that parenting was a tough job to do well. Sometimes salvaging scraps was about the best that could be hoped for.

It hadn't been as jolly an evening as poker night usually was, but had given everyone food for thought.

***

Design Parameters

"But my brother is gay. A flaming homosexual. How on earth is it possible that he won't go straight to hell?"

Ahmad and God had met several times here in heaven, but this was the first time the subject of his brother's sexual orientation had entered one of their conversations.

Today, the two men had just finished a two-hour archery tournament and God was taken aback when the conversation took such a peculiar turn.

"What makes you ask, Ahmad?"

"Ah, well, my brother is only a couple of years younger than I am and he and I grew up competing in archery, so I guess he's crossed my mind in the last couple of hours."

"That also explains why your scores were so much better than mine!" God smiled. "Let's snag those two chairs in the shade, shall we?"

After getting settled and ordering a couple of 7-Ups, God turned back to Ahmad and asked, "So, you're worried that your brother is aging, has remained gay and won't make it to heaven, is that it?"

"This is so embarrassing. What an awful thing for me to be asking you about, but who else would know? Yes, I wonder if we'll ever see each other again. Basheer was such a great boy and young man; my favorite sibling, if I'm honest. But when he 'came out' as a queer man, he was essentially disowned by our family and community; it made seeing him difficult. Most people there assumed he had just signed his passport to hell. Is that true?"

"Phew, Ahmad, you sure know how to paint a guy into a corner, don't you?" God's tone was warmer than his words, but as he ran his hands through his hair, it was obvious that he was choosing his next words carefully.

"You know, when I created humans, I only made two genders; it wasn't a multiple-choice buffet where people could pick and choose. And, from the very beginning, there have been men and women who disregarded my design parameters and indulged in whatever perversions of those designs they could think of.

"As with so many things, balance is the determining factor in the heaven/hell decision. Whatever my personal feelings on substitutions of all kinds, I make every effort to look at the whole picture when making the thumbs up or down decision. Does that make sense to you?"

"Well, do you mean that being gay isn't an automatic disqualifier for heaven?" Ahmad asked hopefully.

"There are a lot of 'ifs,' but yes, a gay person can assuredly get to heaven. One of the problems for many of the other-gendered is that, in their explorations, they have abused children and other vulnerable people to satisfy their own desires. Nobody, straight or gay, gets here if they've sexually abused others, if their partners weren't willing. Now a few abusers, in the rarest of instances, have gotten in after a stretch in purgatory, but I stress the 'few' aspect."

Ahmad gulped before asking, "Why are some people attracted to others of their own sex and others find the whole notion abhorrent? I know there are a lot of theories about it, but what's the truth?"

"You're right about the abundance of theories! And some of them make sense, but the truth is that, if the idea had ever crossed my mind in the design stage, I would have looked for a fix. To be ostracized by families and society is hugely painful, but so is feeling coerced into living a lie. Whether homosexual or transgender issues are biological or emotional, I can't tell you, but they sure complicate a life and weren't a part of my plan.

"Ahmad, your brother has lived a long life, so, in spite of the familial rejections he experienced, he seems to have found enough balance to go on. Not everyone does. I've often wondered if the higher rates of suicide among gays is a cause or an effect of their gender confusion; whether it's all a part of the same wiring problem. Now, I know it's politically correct to say it's all 'natural' and that homosexuality is as normal as heterosexuality, but it wasn't the natural order of things."

"Well, you probably didn't plan for drugs, smoking and a million other things we humans cooked up on earth, either, did you?" Ahmad sounded fairly lighthearted in his query.

"That's putting it mildly!" God laughed. "I've been fascinated from day one at how the simplest design functions can be abused, corrupted and just generally mangled. But a lot of that 'creativity' has also led man to inventions and schools of thought that have helped him to make great strides in many fields. Taking the bad with the good is the only way I can look at it."

"But, about Basheer, will I see him here?" Ahmad was no longer lighthearted, he sounded anguished. "And would my parents be accepting of him?"

"Ahmad, I don't speculate about someone still on earth. What I can tell you is that the smoothed edges everyone experiences here in heaven would certainly apply to your family's acceptance of Basheer. They would see the child they had loved and appreciate the honorable deeds of his adult life. The rest would be mercifully blurred as it is for everyone. My children don't come to heaven for discord, they come for and experience joy and love.

"I'm a little concerned, though that the 'smoothed edges' aspect seems to have failed you a bit, Ahmad. You shouldn't be fretting over your brother's fate; has this been going on for long?"

"Really, it hasn't. I was pretty surprised when it hit me like a hammer as we were on the range. Then, it suddenly felt like I'd been losing sleep over it for months."

"Oh, good! Not good that you got hammered by it of course, but good that it's of such short duration. I imagine the newness of being back on the archery range is what did it and that your usual calm will descend again, soon.

"What do you say, my boy, shall we call it a day?"

The two men embraced before going their separate ways and Ahmad set off with the usual spring back in his step.

***

The Dark and the Light

"Why am I here? That *was* Saint Peter out there, wasn't it? I'm trying to put all the pieces together; you sure look like I'd expect God to look, which would make this heaven, and it's not where I was expecting to end up."

"Because?" prompted God.

"Well, hell, man...look at me. And if you think I *look* like a filthy, tatted banger, you should have seen the way I lived my life!"

"Oh, I have a pretty good record here... " God began as he indicated the yellow legal pad in his hand.

"You may have my sheet," interrupted Sandy, "but that ain't the half of it. My life was one degenerate son-of-a-bitch."

"I have it all, including what you did to your mother. And don't interrupt me again." God's stony voice echoed around the room where they stood.

Sandy blanched and stayed quiet.

"Sander Thomas Dolan, the Third. That doesn't sound like the moniker attached to a street thug, and yet that's what you chose to be. I know you were raised in a good, Catholic family, and I'm curious why you embraced the idea of going to hell for the choices you made?"

"That's it? You don't want to know why I made those *choices*, just my thoughts on choosing hell?"

"Oh, I know all of your turning points and rationalizations. They aren't a part of this discussion. Just tell me your thought process regarding going to hell and not minding the prospect of it."

"Well, first off, I never really took seriously the concept of you, heaven *or* hell. I figured that none of my bros would be in heaven anyway, and I sure didn't need more confrontations with any of my family. Secondly, I just thought that if I was either cremated or fried in a bike pile-up, that would pretty much take care of the fiery hell aspect."

"Well, you figured wrong. If you thought your zip through that crematorium for indigents was as bad as it got, you were dreaming. Having your corpse 'fried' didn't hurt, did it? You were already dead by that point, so you don't get points for having experienced hell. Follow me over here." God ordered, turning and walking to a curtained wall.

Sandy gasped as the drapes opened onto a balcony overlooking a pit.

"Come along," God instructed, "it's not hot from here. "

They stood side-by-side on a perfectly cool balcony with a horrifying panorama spread below and ahead of them. The hell-scape of tortured souls dragging and pushing all manner of smoldering burdens through a landscape of sputtering flames and bubbling lava was punctuated with otherworldly sounds too horrible to bear.

Gagging, Sandy lurched backward.

"That's the preview many people envision to some small degree." God barked, stepping away from the closing drapery. "Their churches or parents may be the ones who plant the seed and usually a seed is all it takes. It has a tendency to keep them decent enough to avoid it as their fate. *You,* on the other hand, mindfully chose and embraced the concept of hell, so as much as it pains me to grant you anything you asked for..."

God pushed down the ominously silent lever on the wall, turned his back and walked toward the waiting woman materializing as Sandy dropped to his reward.

"Thank you for allowing me to be here, I know it's not standard practice." Fiona slumped into God's sheltering embrace as he kept his back to her son's descent into hell.

As he gently walked Fiona out of the room and into his private garden, God murmured soothingly as he helped her settle into a chair. "You are one of the bravest people I've ever encountered," he said while she composed herself, "and, yes it certainly is rare for my children to be allowed to witness anything upsetting here in heaven. I was surprised and conflicted when you approached me about it."

Taking a deep breath, Fiona began, "The term 'closure' is overused on earth when trying to put something finally and permanently behind one, but it certainly applies to this situation. When I somehow knew that Sander would be having his interview with you, everything, even though mercifully muted, came back to me for a moment and I knew I had to ask. I was suddenly certain that I wanted no possibility of ever seeing him after today. Or of having any of the rest of my family subjected to an encounter."

While birds chirped in the idyllic setting, God and Fiona spent a few moments in silence while each reluctantly reviewed a scene they knew too well.

Over twenty years ago, Sander, then thirty-two and knowing that his estranged family would be at their annual St. Patrick's Day picnic and day in the park, had brought his biker gang to ransack their home. He hadn't known that his fifty-year-old mother had stayed home with the flu. The five degenerates took turns raping and pillaging. While Sander only robbed, he made no attempt to call the animals off his mother.

With no mention of Sander, the family doctor was sworn to secrecy as he had treated Fiona. No police reports nor insurance claims were ever filed. The family circle had closed tightly and permanently.

"How do you feel?" God finally ventured.

Breathing deeply, Fiona sounded remarkably strong as she answered, "Free. Gloriously free for the first time since it happened. The fact that he didn't even ask your forgiveness was a gift to me. I can finally consign him to oblivion; I feel sure that he will never concern me again."

"Ah, my dear woman. What a wonderful outcome to a sorry day. And you're right, neither you nor anyone you encounter will ever again have that man cross your minds. Let me accompany you, with that beautiful smile, into the joy that is your renewed heaven." He offered his arm and they walked through the glimmering gates into the light.

***

A Charismatic Guy

"Saint Peter is the only one I've encountered in my 300 years here in heaven who has the honorific still attached to his name. Where are all of the others we read about in the bible?" Erastus and God were up to their knees in a lake whose shores they were clearing of cattails.

"Oh, most of them are here, but the gatekeeper is the only one who uses the title." God struggled for a moment with the muck that was sucking at his sandal. "You were right, barefoot is better." He pulled both of his sandals off and flung them to the shore. "I guess you've noticed by now that I'm not a big fan of titles, but there are times when it makes it easier on all concerned to know *which* Peter you're referring to. He's a pretty distinctive character, isn't he?"

"I'll say. I know he's a favorite of yours, but he's sure an unpredictable fellow!" Erastus was trying to not offend God by asking too many questions about the sentinel at the podium in God's waiting room. He was genuinely curious, though.

God whuffed a bit of cattail fluff from under his nose before replying. "Yes, he is a favorite of mine, I hope it's not as obvious to everyone's eye as to yours. When Peter was born, around the same time Jesus was, he was named Simeon and he later became a simple fisherman. Most of those fellows of that era, the ones involved with Jesus, I mean, are pretty good people. They became enamored with the idea of his being the savior and made great sacrifices for him.

"Many eras have a charismatic guy who shows up on the scene, inspires devotion and, often, new religions. From Zoroaster to Krishna to Martin Luther to Joseph Smith, there's always been someone with the chutzpa to energize armies of followers.

"Jesus was one of those. He and his acolytes happened into a fairly literate and relatively peaceful time, so they had the leisure to travel and really sell the idea of me. He's always seemed abashed that his advocacy of me became, after his death, a canonization of him."

"But, golly, how could that *not* have happened?" Erastus sounded almost anguished at the thought of Jesus' not having achieved his hallowed status. "He was born to a virgin; he was your son! He died on the cross for us, for heaven's sake."

"Ah, child." God came to a stop in the muck and pushed the hair from his face. "It's always so hard for me to speak to Jesus' life without sounding like I'm putting him down. I adore him and would never disparage anything about the way he lived, but I might take issue with some of the myths that arose after his death."

"Such as?" Erastus tried asking without becoming belligerent.

"Well, you mentioned his having died on a cross. The cross has become so firmly entrenched as a symbol of Jesus' life and death that it tends to be forgotten that thousands of Jews and others, over maybe ten centuries, were crucified as a particularly humiliating form of capital punishment; it certainly wasn't unique to him.

"Jesus is widely quoted as having cried out, while hanging on that gruesome device, something along the lines of, 'My God, why have you forsaken me?' You've heard that?" As Erastus nodded, God continued, "And why would I? What kind of a god would, if he had any control at all over earthly matters, have allowed Jesus or anyone else to be tortured? The whole affair was man's doing. I'm so glad that Jesus has always, certainly in his heavenly state, acknowledged that and loved me." God, seeing Erastus' confusion and discomfort, took a deep breath, adopted a big smile and turned the conversation.

"Anyway, back to Peter; he was instrumental in the founding of Christianity, but I guess the thing I first admired about him was his negotiation between those who chose to follow Jesus and the extant Jews. It was a delicate line to walk between two major sects, and he managed it."

"He's a lucky fellow to have you as an advocate." Erastus still sounded less than totally beyond the 'cross' diversion or convinced that Peter was an okay fellow.

God laughed and acknowledged that, yes Peter could be a grouch with an attitude, "But, I just like him! About the time he came to heaven, I was realizing that I needed someone to man the entry besides me. He had kind of a pedigree as the 'keeper of the keys' and he was amenable to the task, so we decided to give it a shot. Use of the 'Saint' part started out kind of kiddingly and just stuck. Like all good friends, we've butted heads now and then, but he's one of my rocks. Does that make sense to you?"

"Yeah, it does; and I like him a little better with the background. Now, I don't know about you, but I'm ready to get out of this mud!"

The two men splashed and slogged to shore and into a clear stream to rinse off.

***

God's Verdict

"Why did you commit suicide?" God asked Fred in this, their initial meeting.

"Yeah, well. This is awkward because I know it's on your list of no-no's, but have you ever just felt so totally beaten that there doesn't seem to be any point in going on?"

"Not really an option I have," sighed God.

"Hadn't thought of it, but I guess that's true, huh? One more thing we all owe you for. Anyway, I'm sorry if I offended you by checking out on my own, but I'm only human, I don't have divine strength and there's no way to describe how totally defeated I was feeling."

"Try."

"Okay. First off, I'm old and everything gets harder every single day. Things that I've always handled myself now have to be farmed out to handymen who don't know shit from Shinola... sorry... I try to be patient and accept their lousy workmanship, but it's wearing. Then... the world changes so fast that I don't know from one day to the next how my phone or TV is going to operate. Don't know if you can appreciate how exhausting and aggravating that is.

"Besides being old, my health is worse every week and I've never been one to run to a doctor for every little thing or take handfuls of pills. I just plain don't feel good anymore and it's overwhelming to think of trying to fix all of it. Especially knowing that, at my age, they'd just be stop-gap fixes.

"My wife, Penny, used to nag me about vitamins and vegetables, but now that she's out of it with Alzheimer's, all of the caregiving is on me. It's not her fault, I know that, but eating my words a dozen times a day to keep from snapping at her is a lousy diet. Watching over her like a three-year-old feels so wrong. The kids wanted to put her in a home to take the load off of me, but we've been together over fifty years and I just couldn't do it.

"Then, a few months ago, Jack died. I... I can't explain it. Jack and I met in high school; in sixty years, we've probably never gone a week without talking and, suddenly, he's gone. Thank God...you, I mean... it was a short illness, which maybe made it easier on him, but I knew I'd never recover. I couldn't even cry with Penny about it, she doesn't know who *I* am, much less remember Jack. I feel completely unmoored. "

"Jack is a good man," interjected God, "I'm glad to have him here."

"Well, I hope to high heaven I get to see him. Hey, I can see *you* just fine, does that mean that if I get in, I'll get my vision back?"

"Back to why you killed yourself." God prodded.

"Well, right there... my vision. I'd gotten so damned blind that I couldn't read, do a crossword, change the oil on my car or much of anything. The specialists had done all they could, and I knew it was just a matter of time before I had to quit driving or kill someone. How...what's there to do if you can't drive or read? They've made my life's favorite activities possible. Except for... well..."

"Sex?" asked God gently.

"Yeah. That was probably the first major loss. I kept it up for longer than some of the guys I know, but to know it will never happen again is just the most demoralizing, humiliating thing I've ever had to live with. It was a huge part of who I was and what my marriage to Penny was.

Even after she got goofy as hell, she was interested and got so confused when I couldn't respond."

The newcomer bent his head, pinched the bridge of his nose and cried.

"Lots of losses." God commiserated.

Sighing, Fred tried to continue. "When I did it, I still had enough money to help the kids with the expense of a good facility for Penny. If I'd had to go into a home, too, the money would be gone in a flash. And for what? So I can sit and stare at a wall I can't see? So I can mourn Jack and Penny and all the others? So my kids have to take responsibility for their old man? What's the point? I've had a great life. I thank you for all the blessings you gave me. Why should the ending be a downhill slide that benefits no one?"

God sighed again. "You've used your blessings wisely and shared them with others. You're a good man, Fred. But this isn't how it was supposed to end. We like to see people trapped in hospital beds with tubes running in all directions and a string of drool falling down their chins."

"WHAA...?! What are you talking about? Are you the Devil?!" Fred interrupted wildly.

"I'm sorry, Fred, this isn't the time for me to be a wise guy about my own frustrations. I apologize. No, I'm not the devil, though it would be easy for people to wonder about that when they look at the contradictions between modern medicine and religion. I can't prevent the suffering that goes on in life and nobody would ever learn anything about themselves or others if they didn't have consequences to their actions. Or, in the case of your poor Penny, if researchers couldn't study her and try to learn how to eradicate some of the worst diseases. It's a complicated and unhappy world down there in many ways. Having religion and science at odds doesn't help.

"But when a person has done his best with what he's been given and has really thought it through, there are worse things than making the last decision for yourself."

"Wow. That sounds like such common sense." marveled Fred.

"Yes, well, some of it does filter in around here." God mused. "Now, Jack is waiting to take you around and Penny will be here before you know it, so go along, my son, and enjoy your reward."

✦✦✦

God's Wet Nurse

"**Y**ou've referred to yourself as having a 'job.' But who could possibly be your boss? Does that mean there's some force larger than you? Where did *you* come from? How do you know what you're supposed to do?"

God had heard some version of those and a trillion other questions since the first caveman got here. One of his own constraints was that he wouldn't lie. Oh, he could skirt around a topic if it would cause unnecessary distress in one of his children, but truth really was the best policy most of the time.

When a sweetly eccentric resident peppered him with so many questions in one chance encounter, he was nonplused. Gert wasn't pushy, just curious.

"The other day," she continued, "I was in a conversation with several others and referred to someone I'd known on earth as having been 'older than God's wet-nurse.' Sorry, but it's an expression I've always used, and it just came out."

God chuckled and assured Gert that he'd heard it before and found it to be pretty amusing.

"But then we started wondering at all of the ramifications involved in the phrase. I mean, it implies that you were born an infant and had human needs for nutrition and care. Which means parents, right?"

"Your guess is as good as mine, Gert. My first conscious memory is of a peaceful feeling of wholeness and contentment. I was about the same 'age' as you see me now. I had an innate, grown-up sense of a job to do and how to accomplish it. There weren't any written instructions or parents guiding me, it was just *in* me. So, I set about creating all of the universes, animals, plants and people. It was challenging and satisfying work."

"Weren't you lonely?"

"You know, I was so busy for so long that I don't remember having been. Maybe by the time I would have felt loneliness, people and animals, all my children, had begun arriving here and our interactions have satisfied me."

"So you really do consider us all your children." marveled Gert." But did you never feel the need of a wife?"

"No, honestly, I haven't. I guess I'm what people would call an asexual being; I enjoy most of my interactions with the men and women here, but I never feel the kind of attraction that mortal men need to feel to keep procreation going. I'm really fulfilled by the relationships we all have here; they're stimulating, informative and a lot of fun!"

Gert laughed, "And all of us who interact with you know that you have your moods and preferences; they're part of what make us so comfortable with you rather than seeing you as an unapproachable deity. You do a really good job of passing as human!"

***

Sixth Commandment
You Shall Not Murder

The evening's poker game had gone off without a hitch. Everyone had shared about equally in the pot and, as he tended bar, Carl told a tale of a guy in Louisiana who had beat a murder rap. Carl took his chair as Ruby noted that this was an obvious segue for the sixth commandment discussion if everyone was up for it. They all agreed and started off the discussion obviously expecting it to be wrapped up quickly.

"Well, for Pete's sake! How can anyone make a case *for* murder? That commandment seems like an open and shut case, doesn't it?" Ruby looked around at everyone.

But, shifting in his seat by the fire, Carl cleared his throat and took exception.

"Well, we all know there are all sorts of legal definitions for killing somebody; manslaughter, self-defense, accidental; there are a lot of ways to say there's a dead body to be accounted for. To me, 'murder' means something purposeful, planned and un-repented, does that sound about right?" Carl looked to God.

God massaged his head lightly before answering. "It's a thorny topic. Un-repented may not always be accurate; if someone kills in a moment of passion, he may well have remorse over it, but his victim is still just as dead.

"There *are* some 'murderers' in heaven because I have access to the whole picture of a person's life; information that judges, juries and the press don't have or can't consider. 'Mitigating circumstances' is legalese, but it's a much broader parameter for me than for those on earth."

Fausto looked troubled. "But killing on purpose; isn't that someone appointing himself to do *your* job?"

"Ahh, except that I don't kill anyone, remember? I don't save people on earth or protect their crops or kill them. I'm hands-off until they get here."

"What about sending them to hell? Doesn't that count as killing them?" Fausto persisted.

God laughed lightly and retorted, "Boy, you're full of beans, tonight, aren't you? Those who end up in hell are guilty of capital crimes by *my* standard. I don't concern myself with their well-being. Others, whose crimes are on my borderline, have the option of reforming themselves in purgatory, but they have to make the effort. A few murderers make it out of purgatory in pretty short order. Some long before their victims do, if *they* do at all.

"Not all 'victims' are innocent. Many, through their choices, have brought onto themselves death at the hands of their fellow man. Except for man's laws, many of us would cheer some vigilante justice now and then.

"And, certainly, there have to be laws on earth. It's hard enough to maintain some sort of civility among an imperfect populace even with structuring frameworks in place. It's my job to balance the scales here." God winked at Fausto and asked, "You want to take over the job?"

Hasty waving of hands and echoes of "Not me!" bounced around the group.

It had not been the most cheerful evening the group had experienced together, and they were all ready to get some shut-eye. Goodnights were loving, though; they all appreciated the chance for some probing conversation now and then.

***

Caveman Mentality

Richard and God were part of a big crew repairing and painting the playground equipment in one of heaven's parks. For a lot of the guys who had always liked working with tools and their hands, it was a wonderful way to spend a few days with others who shared similar interests.

"This is more like it!" exulted Richard as he and God plopped themselves in the shade waiting for a first coat of paint to dry.

God laughed and agreed it was the best part of the job.

"That guy who's resetting all of the swing sets is amazing," Richard began "I don't think I've ever seen anyone with that physical strength. I started to ask you if he was a caveman or something, and it occurred to me that I've never seen anyone here from that long ago. But they must be here, right?"

"Oh, sure, no matter how old or primitive the civilization, they're all here. But I'm not surprised you wouldn't have seen them. Like everyone else, they tend to stay among those who have the same reference points, habits and sensibilities as they have. And for the most part, those from the really ancient past are big on the everlasting naps.

"If they were from the actual caveman era, they've all long since nodded off to eternal rest. Their lives were so simple that it didn't take long for their interest in each other to peter out.

"A few years ago, a fellow named Kushim put in an appearance in the modern city of Aleppo. He'd been a citizen of the region of Levant in around 1500 BC, but nothing exists there today that indicates 'home' to him. Poor fellow awoke from a long nap and apparently thought something that landed him in modern times. Luckily, I felt it happen and was able to intercept him very quickly.

"We strolled around and chatted for a short time, but he was disoriented and most eager to get back home to those he recognized as being 'his' people."

Richard was spellbound by God's story. "Well, I know that Kushim and I, or my equivalent in Syria, could have communicated, but what on earth could we have had in common enough to even put together a conversation? I can't imagine being so totally out of your element. It sounds terrifying."

"Yes, I suspect that's just how he felt, too. He came from a place and era when an alphabet was created, but, of course, that didn't filter down to the commoners for a long time, so finding himself among people who had lived into the computer era would have been petrifying for such a simple fellow as Kushim is. In his era, survival took most of people's time and energy, so, except for the muckety-mucks, they had pretty simple thought processes and interests. He was overwhelmed and confused at finding himself here. Not the feelings I want for any of my children."

"So, you got him back to where he came from?" Richard asked.

"Yes. We spent a short time together... I hadn't seen him since he first arrived, so it was calming for him and good for me to reconnect, but he wanted outta there in the worst way. When he got back to his own era, he became quite a celebrity for a short time and then went back to napping. I imagine he was beyond exhausted by his inadvertent adventure, poor soul."

"How many people would have been up and around to celebrate Kushim? I'd think most of such a simple era would have long since opted for napping."

"You're right, Richard, there were few out and about, but they were wowed by his step into the unknown. It's only been in the last few thousand years that people have chosen fewer permanent naps. When people began to know their family history and be able to make connections with multiple generations, the pleasures of heaven became more long-lasting. As time went on, friendship circles widened, too. It's more stimulating when you can interact with more and different people.

"Of course, there are always a few people in any civilization or time who really do just 'vant to be alone' to quote the famous Ms. Garbo. Some wake refreshed and interested in mingling and others just want to call it a night.

"Speaking of which, what do you think of getting to the second coat of this paint tomorrow?"

The two hammered lids down tight, left the rinsed brushes and rollers to dry and set off for the evening.

***

The Oldest Profession

"Surely, you don't think it was my idea of a good choice?!" Lena was immediately defensive when God asked her about the profession she'd spent several years in. Their meeting, as Lena entered God's chamber, had gotten off to a rocky start.

"Well, I guess that's really what I'm asking you. From here, it looked like you had other options, but I do understand that things don't always look the same on the ground." God's tone was soothing as he tried to keep the conversation from going off the rails. "Did you feel trapped into prostitution?"

"Looking back on it;" Lena was obviously trying to calm her emotions; "no, I wasn't trapped the way some were. There were so many kids with drug issues who were a pimp's delight. They were certainly a lot more 'trapped' than I was. Basically, I guess I was just lazy. It's probably a justification, but I was so beat up by that awful first marriage that, when the first unplanned trick went so easily, I thought, hell, why go back to clerking?"

"Wasn't it hard to explain to your family?" God knew the answer but wanted Lena to work it out.

"Pshh. They'd never approved of the husband but approved even less of a divorce. There wasn't much I could do to please them, so I'd quit trying by then. I don't think they wanted to know what was happening in my life, so that's what we all got."

"You didn't have any moral struggles over what you were doing? Your family may not have been the most supportive one, but you were raised pretty well from what I see here." God ruffled the lined yellow pages.

"No, I can't blame anyone but myself for deciding to whore for a few years. If I'd had some education or a career to fall back on, I might have. But the money was good and I was lucky to have never gotten the hell beat out of me the way some women did. So... was it a fatal error? Am I going to hell for it?"

God puffed his cheeks and blew out a sigh. "Lena, what you did was an unsavory choice and pretty universally damned. But, at its core, it was a business decision you made that really harmed no one. You don't seem to have ever robbed any of the guys who bought your services or blackmailed any of the married ones. I've seen a lot worse behavior in some bankers. Your life before and after those years was about as average as any. So, no, you won't go to hell, it takes some really egregious stuff to end up there."

God rose and walked Lena to the gates leading to heaven. As he cordially waved her through and closed the gate he'd held for her, he was unsettled at the awkward feeling he had. There were certainly trillions of worse people who had showed up here and selling oneself wasn't limited to call-girls; plenty of pinstriped shysters should have 'whore' stamped on their foreheads.

Prostitution is just such a personal, intimate activity that it was always a little unnerving to encounter a practitioner.

***

One Bad Summer

"Well, that's nice to hear!" God was opening the door to welcome Ned to his private reception area as he heard Ned and Saint Peter sharing a laugh as they waved goodbye.

"He seems like a really nice guy," grinned Ned. "You can't imagine how surprised I was to see him actually greeting new arrivals from his podium!"

"You must be the nice guy, Ned, Pete can be a little prickly now and then." God was laughing as he indicated a chair for Ned. "So, welcome to heaven! This is a big day, huh? I always get such a kick out of welcoming my children home..." God was interrupted by Ned.

"Are you really sure about me? I may not be who or what you think I am, and I'd hate to get settled in and then be dragged off and sent to hell if you found out."

"Holy smoke, Ned. Tell me what has you so concerned."

"OK, this is kind of a long story, but if I don't get it off my chest, I'll be looking over my shoulder for the rest of this life, too, and I'm exhausted by it.

"Two things I did in my teens have eaten at me for my whole life. I 'straightened up and flew right' as my Dad would have said, but I always felt that I was hiding the real me, so I'd like to tell you the whole thing, if that's alright." God nodded and swept his open palm in a 'go right ahead' gesture.

"We always lived in an area that got a lot of seasonal visitors and some of those people had cabins that were only used when the ski slopes were open. To us, those folks were 'rich,' which I realize, looking back on it, was hogwash, but that's how it looked to a kid. One summer when I was about thirteen, a couple of friends had the bright idea that we should break into a few of those cabins and see what we could find. I was so scared I almost peed myself, but I jumped right in and off we went. We weren't too destructive, but we did take a few oddball things before setting off for the next one.

"Why we didn't get caught, I can't tell you. We were so damned stupid. Back then, nobody had security cameras or anything of the sort, so I guess that saved us. That was bad enough, but the worst came later that same summer.

"A couple of doors down from one of the kids' houses, someone had put a 'missing' flyer on a phone pole. There was a blurry photo of a cat and a phone number below, begging for information. The three of us went back to the house of the guy who lived nearby and called the number from the flyer. He told the woman who answered that the cat was dead in the street and named a street one block over. We ran over there and watched through some bushes as the poor woman looked everywhere for her pet. Watching her, I wished I was dead.

"I swear to you that I have never again in my life done anything so abhorrent, but those two incidents have haunted me." Ned was shaking and on the verge of tears. God allowed a silence to settle before responding.

"Ned, first, while you calm yourself, I want you to know that your actions aren't going to send you to hell. It sounds like you've punished yourself more than adequately.

"While the conduct of you and your friends certainly called for a good butt-busting, you weren't caught, so it didn't happen. You were blessed with good parents who just happened to miss out on that summer's bad deeds. The emotional lessons you learned served you well for your whole life though, didn't they?"

"Oh, man. That's an understatement. I imagine the specter of that summer is what kept me on the straight and narrow; I always felt like a fraud, though, like, if people had known the real me, they'd drop me like a hot potato.

"I've wondered if my Dad's job transfer and our move to another state during the following winter helped me. I wasn't tempted to keep hanging out with the kids who knew how rotten I was, so I didn't have to live down to their expectations.

"And what about those other boys? I never wanted to look back anyway, but I did wonder a few times if they leveled out too, or if they went on to lives of serious crime."

"Boy, Ned, you've given this... what? ... more than sixty years of thought? And pretty much covered all the bases, I'd say. Now, you obviously needed to get this off your chest and I'm glad to have been here for you. But I know every bad and good deed you've ever done and am perfectly comfortable in telling you the good far, far outweighs the bad. Hell has never been even a glimmer on your horizon. A part of the reason for childhood is to learn lessons that inform your choices as you move through life and you were a quick study!"

"What happened to that poor woman and her cat? I feel like an idiot for even asking; I can't even imagine what all you have to keep up with."

God smiled as he said, "When she arrived home, Mrs. Harris found her cat yowling on the back porch. She was so thrilled and relieved to have him safely home that she looked at the whole incident as kind of a 'God' moment and let it go."

"Wow! What great news! You can't know how that pleases me." Ned was beaming from ear to ear. "She won't recognize me in heaven and chew me a new one, will she?"

"No, Ned. And you're going to be so much more relaxed than you've ever allowed yourself to be before. Heaven has no grudges and bad memories are softened to the point that they rarely surface. As to those childhood friends, one went on to be almost as good a guy as you while the other lived a pretty unsavory life. But if you should ever run into either of them, only good memories will remain, so no more looking over your shoulder, okay?"

The two men laughed as God walked Ned to the gates and his unburdened future.

***

A Matter of Semantics

"The thing about praying is it's so deeply ingrained into most of us that we do it before even thinking about it. How on earth, would you ever get people to stop *praying?*" Allen and God were chatting while organizing a section of books in one of heaven's libraries.

God paused with a few books in the crook of his arm as he thought about Allen's question. "There's nothing inherently wrong with praying. When one hears a chorus of birdsong first thing in the morning and says a quick prayer of joyful thanks, it gets their day off to a great start. It's food for the soul.

"People don't usually see that prayer as a communion with their soul, though. And it is their most direct connection to the part of me that resides in them.

"I've been astounded for millennia at man's determination to keep praying in traditional modes when those prayers are, at least as often as not, thrown back in his face."

"Well, that's sure true," Allen began, "After I got here to heaven, I looked back objectively at some of the prayers I'd offered on earth and, whether they were of the knee-jerk 'please don't let this car fall off the lift' variety or the soul-wrenching 'please let my dog live through this' heartbreakers, their success rates were beyond dismal."

"You just spoke the magic word, Allen. Prayers can certainly be soul-wrenching. The soul is man's connection to me, but it doesn't answer prayers. It's a tool I left with every human; it helps you to reason your way through things like right, wrong, honest or cowardly and using or disregarding your common sense. Knowing those distinctions is crucial to living a decent, productive life. But if, when conversing with your soul, you believe you're praying to a God who has a magic wand and is waiting to fulfill your requests, you stand a very good chance of being disappointed.

"Your example of the car on the lift, for instance. If, before standing under it, you had consulted with your soul, even through prayer, about its stability and the car's proper placement, you might have heard your common sense advise you to check that the lift arms were locked. You will not experience a heavenly intervention. The car may fall and miss you, but that's a fluke of good fortune or a miracle, not me stepping into the garage."

"You're not behind miracles either?" Allen asked as he situated the last book from his pile.

"No... they *do* happen, but they genuinely *are* random acts of dumb luck. I know that's not a very spiritual way to look at them, but I don't intervene in earthly matters for good *or* for ill. I don't cause Jesus' face to appear in the margarine tub any more than I take a life.

"Praying to me to spare a life doesn't help. And, if the person *does* die, it can make the one who did all the praying feel that I either didn't hear them or didn't care, which can lead to anger and a re-examination of whether or not one even believes in me."

Allen took a few moments to process God's comments before replying, "Wow, if looked at in that light, praying to you rather than examining the situation with my soul could actually be detrimental to my faith. I could end up feeling deserted in my time of extreme need."

"Yes, it's kind of a matter of semantics, isn't it? If one uses the word 'praying' to denote 'asking for divine intervention,' he may be disappointed... unless luck steps in. But if he interprets 'praying' as looking to his soul, his wiser self, for calm and guidance, he may find the strength to handle whatever comes."

God put his last book on its shelf and turned to Allen. "I'm glad we got the books taken care of; always good to put a check mark beside something, isn't it?" Allen laughed and the two men stepped out into the light.

***

Light the Lamp

"Ah, Mickey; welcome to heaven!" God had arranged to meet this new arrival in the empty stands of heaven's hockey rink and stepped down the couple of tiers to greet him at ground level with a paternal embrace.

"You look just like God! Is this heaven?" The man smiled at God as they looked each other over.

"Yes, Mickey and I'm so happy you're here. What do you think of our hockey facility? Does it look like a place you'll enjoy playing?" God asked as he led them up to the nosebleed section and got the two of them settled on the top bench.

Mickey looked around at the arena and smiled widely. "Well, sir, I'm not a player, but I sure know how to take care of the towels and lockers! You know, I'm sort of disabled in some ways, but I'm a steady worker and I loved being a dressing room attendant; I did it for thirty years."

"You're very modest for someone who's in the Alberta Hall of Fame and actually met the Queen of England!

"And, Mickey, this *is* heaven; did you notice how effortlessly you ascended the bleachers? From here on, your Down Syndrome will be entirely your call. You can show the signs of it or not."

Mickey stood up abruptly. Glancing at God first, he turned and hesitantly descended to the next-to-last step where he paused and jumped to the ground, landing on both feet. Jubilantly, Mickey whirled and galloped back up to a cheering God. Amid much backslapping, they laughed and hugged for a moment. After getting re-settled, God explained to Mickey that his family and friends might see him at first as they had known him on earth, but as they acclimated to his slightly more refined appearance, they wouldn't remember his earthly looks if he'd prefer they didn't.

"It's your call, Mickey. Your family did a wonderful job of raising you to be proud of yourself just as you were. Then, once you became such a valued mascot for the professional hockey team, you achieved a measure of fame that you may want to hang onto. Heaven is all about options, and there's no hurry at all to make any decisions."

After a long, melancholy pause, Mickey asked, "But am I still dumb?"

God cupped both hands to Mickey's middle-aged but still childlike face. "Oh, my child, you're not dumb, no matter what some of earth's crueler people may have made you think. While Down's people do tend to the lower end of earth's IQ scales, there are plenty of people down there a lot dumber than you are. And, just like your hockey employers, heaven knows how to bring out the very best in our people. That's why I suggested that you might be excited about getting on the ice with a stick, yourself. You might just become the next Beauty...is that the term I'm looking for? We have teams at every level and they're always happy to welcome in a new Wayne Gretzky wannabe." Mickey's delighted laughter gladdened God's heart.

"Now, Mickey, let's take a walk down those steps. You have family and friends waiting outside that bright red 'exit' sign and they're too excited to wait much longer!"

***

Cold and Hot

"So, how were the four years you lived after the death of your husband?" God and Tilda were standing in a beautiful but chilly room for her interview.

"Oh, they were okay, I guess. I didn't know I had cancer until I was almost dead, which was doubtless better than spending years treating it. I had hoped that, after Gene was gone, I might marry again, but it probably worked out as well that I didn't."

God was uncharacteristically reserved in this audience. He hesitated before asking; "Tell me about Gene's death and the time leading up to it."

"Well, he'd been senile for a couple of years before he died, so they were pretty lonely years for me. Physically, he was in surprisingly good shape, but had to be watched like a toddler, so it was draining. His doctor didn't feel that a facility was called for, so even though we had insurance, we didn't have a referral. It all made life very limited."

"Um hmm. How was it for Gene? Was he on medication for the dementia? Were you able to keep him happy in his condition? How was *his* quality of life?"

"Golly, it's so cold in here, is all of heaven this nippy?" Tilda asked as she rubbed her arms and her eyes roamed around the vast room that looked like an ornate church.

"About Gene?" God prompted.

After a long silence, Tilda hissed, with a tone of defiance, "You *know* all those answers, don't you? Why are you setting a trap for me?"

All subterfuge behind him, God retorted: "I believe you laid your own trap, Tilda. You were the younger, healthier one in that marriage and you just plain got angry with having to be a caregiver, didn't you?

"You nursed your grievances against Gene until you convinced yourself that *you* were the wronged one. Gene's doctor never diagnosed dementia, did he? You basically began gaslighting Gene and, due to his age rather than real senility, he was an easy mark. How am I doing, so far?"

"*My* life was running out, too! As far as I knew, I could have had another twenty years ahead of me! And I was supposed to spend them with a doddering old fool who couldn't help with *anything*?!"

"With anything except the money, right? You had to outlive Gene to lay your hands on any of that complicated trust fund and if you'd had the decency to just divorce him, it would all have gone to his kids and grandkids, isn't that how it worked?"

"Well, you've got it all figured out, haven't you? It must be nice to live up here, away from any of the pressures of real life! And expect the rest of us to live up to *your* standards. I guess you're going to blame me for the fact that Gene went out in the freezing cold to look for that scroungy old dog of his. The dog was older and dumber than Gene, if that's possible, and it was *not* my fault that they both froze to death!"

Tilda had worked herself into a frenzy which had warmed her considerably.

"Before you leave," God intoned, "I want you to be 100% clear on the fact that I know all about the sleeping pills and the locked doors. I know how carefully you planned the details of both Gene and the poor old dog's deaths. *And* I know that you never felt a moment's shame or regret over the deaths you caused out of pure greed. You are an abhorrent woman and I can assure you that your eternity will be significantly warmer than this room."

With that, God pushed down the lever that squealed as Tilda dropped into Satan's kingdom. He rarely felt any satisfaction with bringing hell into the picture, but God sometimes felt, as he did now, that a wrong had been righted.

***

Goose and Gander

"**Y**eah, but weren't there times when you'd have liked to be a reverse polygamist and have men around for different purposes?" Darcie giggled as she made the proposal in response to Opal's comment. "One could take care of the car, one could do the barbecuing, and one (or more!) could take care of me!"

"Oh, you're awful!" Janet howled as wine spurted from her nose.

The three women had stayed on in one of heaven's meeting rooms after the Bunco tournament ended and were making a dent in the club's wine cellar.

"Oh, Lordy," groaned Opal. "Ward is a good husband and I love him, but three or four of them? God save me! One of the best things about heaven is that we don't have to be together 24/7 the way we did in his retirement years. I love the fact that we can go for long stretches of time without seeing each other. Then, when we both really want to share some time together, it's so natural and fun.

No suspicions or hurt feelings, it's great. But to be juggling several of them? No thanks."

Janet spoke up and asked, "Did either of you ever live around polygamists?"

"Gosh, no, I didn't realize there were still any *in* the United States. And what on earth would you call that kind of marriage if Darci managed to snare several husbands?" Opal looked at the others.

"Oh, they're there, alright, and I believe the multiple husbands would be called polyandry." Darci began, "My husband's job had us moving around in Arizona and Utah for quite a while and we got to know lots of regular Mormons and experienced a few of the FLDS variety."

"Wow. I'm fascinated," began Janet, "What's the difference between 'regular' and 'FLDS'?"

Darci refilled her glass and asked; "Do either of you remember back in the early 2000's, I think it was, when a fellow named Warren Jeffs was all over the news for being on the run from rape convictions in a couple of states? He had several underage wives, I think." The others nodded and spent a few minutes remembering and organizing the bits of stories they'd heard.

"Well, Jeffs was FLDS, which stands for 'Fundamentalist Latter Day Saints' or the branch that still practices polygamy. It's illegal now, but certainly not unpracticed. 'Regular' Mormons are, in my experience, a nice bunch of people; there are rotten ones, too, of course, but isn't that true of any of our religions? Oh, and they raise the most polite and delightful children you can imagine. Even the 'regular' ones, nice as they are, socialize mostly with other Mormons, but the fundamentalists are really loners.

"Bob and I used to go to the occasional yard sale or estate auction way out in the boonies and it wasn't unusual to see a guy there with a few wives trailing behind him in their distinctive, old fashioned and very modest dresses. It was a unique experience."

"But where did they live?" Opal asked, " did they really all live in one house? For all the world to see?"

"Oh, I'm sure they did. There were many houses in those areas which had obviously been built to accommodate the polygamist lifestyle. By the time we lived there, most were used for single families, but if houses were far enough out of town, that's probably where the polygamists we encountered lived."

Just then, the women heard footsteps in the entry hall. "Oh! There are people in here!" God greeted them. "I saw lights on and was just going to flip them off."

"You poor thing, are you filling in for the night watchman?" asked one of the gals.

God laughed and wandered to the table. "I don't suppose there's an extra glass?" he asked as one was produced and poured for him.

"This is great timing," Janet began, "We were just discussing polygamy, or in Darci's case, polyandry." Everyone whooped as God fixed his gaze on Darci.

"Golly, I can't imagine how something like that would have escaped my notice, Darci. I only remember Bob; how many other husbands did I miss?"

Laughing, Darci assured God that he hadn't overlooked a harem of husbands, Bob was it. "These bats are just teasing me." She swore while another round of giggling circled the table.

"Well, that's a peculiar topic for such a staid group of ladies to have happened on. If I'm intruding..." God was interrupted by a chorus of 'Oh, no, no's and settled back into his chair.

"No, your timing is perfect. We were discussing polygamy and were surprised when Darci told us that, at least as of twenty or so years ago, it was still being practiced in our country. How is that possible? It seems almost primitive."

"Actually," replied God, "that's a darned good description of polygyny, or the taking of multiple wives. It has happened sporadically through history, but except for a few places in Africa, it's usually been almost shunned. Some struggling societies wanted men to have more wives and children to work the fields, but it didn't last long in most places."

"But what about the Mormons?" Opal asked, "Wasn't it a foundation of their religion?"

"I guess you could say that, but you have to also remember what a young religion Mormonism really is. It was only founded in 1830 and, as far as polygamy is concerned, that was suspended as an official practice in 1890, so its heyday was only a sixty-year span.

"Today's LDS members certainly have a strong set of beliefs, but they're generally as civic-minded and good a group of people as you could hope to find. While the fundamentalists strive to keep polygamy alive, it really affects only a minuscule number of people.

"It's just such a scandalous idea that it gets a lot more than its share of attention. Like the attention in this little group. None of you were Mormon, right?"

"No, although Darci did have experiences with some who were."

"And," put in Darci, "I've seen several Mormon friends here, so I know they're as likely as anyone else to get to heaven, right?" She turned to God.

"Certainly! I judge people much more by their actions than anything else, no matter what their religion was or what they believed on earth. But nobody's told me how this discussion ended up on polygamy... any takers?"

A nervous titter rattled among the women before one brave soul ventured..."Um, well we were joking around about the pros and cons of polyandry." More giggles.

"OKAY then!" God stood abruptly, looked merrily around the group and hooted, "I'm outta here! You gals have a rollicking time and don't forget to turn the lights out!"

Laughter ensued as God turned on his heel and hustled from the building.

***

Old Habits

The venerable woman was sputtering with alternating defiance and fear. "Well then, fine, if you want to send a poor anciana to hell for trying to take care of herself, just go right ahead!"

God was struggling to keep a straight face as he escorted the elderly American-Mexican woman to some comfortable seating to begin her interview. The lady had arrived ready for battle. Saint Peter had apparently taken the brunt of her temper and it tickled God to have seen Pete cowed; it didn't happen very often.

As the stream of agitated chatter jangled on, God would have challenged any speaker in any tongue to have kept up.

"Señora, please... sit and take a deep breath. There's a glass of iced tea right next to you, there." After a calming, quiet few minutes, the angry fusillade of words had ceased, but the defiance was still evident in her posture and flashing eyes.

"Now, my dear, tell me why you're angry and afraid; why do you seem so sure you're headed for hell?"

"Afraid?! No! I'm not *afraid!* After the life I lived, the only thing you could scare me with is a threat to any of my family! Hell is for sinners, so I can face it if I have to."

God waited for the inevitable calm to fall, but it took a while. Finally, Elena sipped from her tea and gave God a little kinder look and began to speak. "You know all of this don't you? You were with me every moment and you know that I had to steal from the first time I walked. If my parents hadn't taught each of their 11 children to pick pockets and pilfer from store shelves, they could never have fed us, much less gotten us to a new life hundreds of miles north of the border. Don't you remember how desperate our lives were?" Her indignant agitation had begun to sound more pleading.

"Yes, Elena, I remember it all. And I know how hard your parents worked to provide for their family. Even the first few years in your new country were a hard, hand-to-mouth existence, weren't they? Being among the oldest of all those siblings put even more pressure on you, didn't it?"

Suddenly, the rigid posture crumpled and the sobs began. God sat quietly, patting her hand while the enormous release both drained and liberated the woman. Finally, in a gentle old voice, Elena began... "My youngest sisters and brothers were the responsibility of us older ones. Whether or not they ate, had clothes to wear or were tended to when sick or injured. Even when we were children ourselves, we weren't allowed to be. Mama grew what she could, cooked what there was and, with the cleaning, it was a full-time job.

"It was never as hard in California, but it took a while to realize it, so I kept helping to provide in the only way I knew. I felt kind of guilty having as much as I did when I knew so many had nothing. My stealing didn't help *them*, did it!" Here was the first levity in her lovely laugh. "We didn't have much English and, really, I never was comfortable speaking it even as I had children of my own. I know that made my adjustment harder than it might have been."

God waited for a moment before replying, "You did a wonderful job with your children, Elena. They and your grandchildren must have made you very proud."

"Yes, I had married a wonderful young man who was born in El Norte and had both languages, so life was never again quite as hard." After a long uncomfortable pause, Elena continued. "We were faithful churchgoers and I confessed to the priest a few times about my compulsive shoplifting, but he wasn't very forgiving. He shamed me. I wouldn't have confessed it if I wasn't already ashamed of it!

"Until the end of my life, I stole everything I could get away with. At first, I think it was just habit, but then there was kind of a feeling of defiance in my taking a few cigarettes out of someone else's pack; like: 'You think I couldn't get along on my own if I had to? Watch this!'"

"It's a shameful habit, I know that, but I just couldn't stop even when I tried a few times. I always knew I might end up in hell, but I guess I thought I was tough enough to bear it. Now... I don't know. I've been so weak and sick; I don't know how much fight is left in me."

"Elena, my dear daughter. If punishing little sins such as you committed was the reason for hell, it would long since have been packed to the rafters. You spent many years and much penance in atoning for your compulsion. You were a good friend to many and a wonderful woman in multiple ways. What kind of an ogre would I be if I condemned you to punishment for all eternity?

"And the best news is that when you leave this chamber, you will be the healthiest you've ever been! My children enter heaven glowing with the well-being and strength to enjoy every moment."

Rising and holding his hand out to Elena, God laughed gently and told her he was happy to welcome her to heaven and would be honored if she allowed him to accompany her to the pearly gates. "They're just over here and you have a huge contingent of family and friends waiting beyond them."

Elena patted God's hand as she took it and cooed; "Ah mijo, you are the father we have all dreamed of."

***

Seventh Commandment
You Shall Not Commit Adultery

God had had some pressing business the month before, so the group had missed a regularly scheduled poker game. "I'm ridiculously pleased to see all of you!" Fausto announced.

"I know, isn't it funny how important these get-togethers have become?" Carl chimed in.

Ruby, who had drawn the bartending gig, laughed as she dumped ice into a silver bucket, "It's such a constant delight getting together with the three of you that I feel a little disoriented when it's off the calendar."

As they took their seats and Carl began showing off his cardsmanship, Fausto turned to an uncharacteristically subdued God and asked if everything was alright.

"Oh, sorry, I guess I brought the office home with me. One winning hand and I'll be back in the swing." God really did sound a little off key and the eyes darting around the table confirmed that they all felt it.

Later, as they assumed their post-game chatting positions around the fire, Ruby asked God if he wanted to share what was obviously still eating him.

"Oh," grumbled God, mussing his hair, "I had a long talk today with a fellow who wanted to know if the affair that had broken up his marriage on earth would be classified as 'adultery.' The guy's 'husband' had been the cheater."

A collective "oof" woofed out. An unusual reticence settled on the group.

"Even though I didn't write the seventh or any of the other commandments," God began, "I sure feel some empathy right now for the guy who did. He must be spinning to realize what the term 'marriage' has come to encompass. Polygamy and homosexuality have been around since forever; then divorce came along and meant battalions of 'exes' and 'seconds' everywhere." As he sighed, what may have been despair colored God's tone.

"I had no idea where man would go with his iterations of 'civilization' over the eons, but I've got to hand it to him, he can sure surprise me now and then. I've adapted and rolled with all of it, but this really is one for the books."

Ruby, sitting closest to God, reached over and patted his arm. 'I'm sorry; it's obviously unhorsed you."

"Thanks, Ruby. Who knew that 'loving your fellow man' meant marrying him, huh? We'll all adapt, but it seems like... oh, nothing's *ever* stayed the same, of course, but it seems like there's zero time to adapt to one change before it's thrown off and there's something newer in its place.

"Adultery, like any other form of cheating is wrong. Why should anyone need for me to tell them that?" God continued in a, for him, disjointed stream-of-consciousness ramble, "Nobody wants to see a marriage end; there were vows exchanged which are broken by divorce, but would society rather see people suffer through 'til death do them part' if a couple are abusing or ignoring their vows?

"If you've made a commitment that you're unable to honor, whether it's to coaching you child's gymnastics team or to your marriage partner, then you need to do the honorable thing by admitting your mistake and untangling from the situation as helpfully and kindly as possible. Gay or straight, honor shouldn't be a hard concept to get; don't make promises you can't keep is pretty basic. I don't know, do you think I'm getting old?"

Before anyone came up with a clever rejoinder, God stood and quietly said, "I'm so grateful to you all for being here tonight. Your love and support have helped me to regain some of my equilibrium. I still don't have an answer for the guy who asked that damn-fool question, but at least I can mull it over now without sputtering.

"I'll see you all next month, I'm going for a long walk; good night, my friends."

"Don't know about you two, but I'm glad these 'commandment' talks are almost over with," groused Carl, after they watched God disappear into a dimmer light than usual, "They often seem to turn dark, don't they? I mean, this didn't even start out as one, so I guess it's just as well that we used God's pickle to get another one out of the way."

"Yes," nodded Fausto, "I agree that they're somewhat unnerving. It seemed like a good idea at the time, but I'm over it. How about you, Ruby?"

In an exaggerated, conspiratorial tone, Ruby whispered, "How about if, the next time we feel we need to have one, we just roll the last three all into one chat and be done with it? Think we could make that fly?"

They all laughed and tossed the idea around on their way out into the evening air.

***

The Messiah... or Not

"Hey! Isn't that Leonard Bernstein playing the piano?" Terry stretched onto his toes to get a peek over St. Peter's shoulder. Pete ignored the question and gestured again at the door awaiting Terry's entry. "Don't keep him waiting." advised the gatekeeper.

Fumbling his way into God's presence, Terry's anticipation felt subtly muted.

"You look confused," God smiled. "do you think you're in the wrong place?"

"Huh? Oh, damn, I sure hope not! Sorry, I didn't mean to greet you that way. You're right, though, I am confused. Was that really Leonard Bernstein playing piano in the entry?"

"Probably," replied God; "he and several of the other musicians here like to play out there on a regular basis. They've all commented on how they enjoy the soaring acoustics. Adds a nice touch, don't you think?"

"So... so, he *lives* here? He's not hired?" Terry's confusion had increased.

God laughed and assured Terry that there were no hired hands around.

"But, he's Jewish, isn't he?" Terry's voice and expression had become more befuddled. "Jews don't believe in Christ, do they? I don't understand; I thought that belief in Christ was pretty much a requirement for admittance to heaven."

"So, you think I should round them all up and say 'Sorry, my bad, you all were supposed to have gone to hell. The down shaft is over there.'"

"No, no, I wouldn't want to see that, but it's essentially what I've heard all my life... those who didn't believe in Christ wouldn't get to heaven. Is that not the case? I don't understand."

"Well, Terry, I don't either." God indicated a couple of chairs and the two men had a seat. "You know," he continued, "the Jews were around and believing in me long before Christ appeared in *any* religion. It really isn't in my wheelhouse to keep track of the beliefs of all the sects, denominations and whatever are out there."

"Are you *kidding* me?!" Terry was incredulous. "Are you saying that you don't know *everything about everything?* I'm stupefied."

"I know the truth and I know what people have felt, said and done by the time they arrive here. If I really sit down and think about it, I probably *do* know all the nuts and bolts of every religion. But I have a pretty full plate and try to save room for the most important stuff. Which, at the moment, is you.

"You believe in Christ," God continued; "and that's apparently worked out well for you. Your life has been a good one and all I would ask of you at this juncture is that you accept every person you encounter here as having been found, *by me*, worthy. Worthy of your respect for a life well-lived. You will find it easier than you think to put aside any prejudices you have if you accept everyone here as a soulmate in God. Enjoy and learn from the unique aspects of each one you meet and embrace them as I have embraced you.

"Depending on the routes you choose to explore here in heaven, you will come across people of every religion you can think of and even more you never knew existed. Specific beliefs aren't required for admission; decent morals and intentions are more important to me.

"I didn't invent religion, you know." God thought he had ended the conversation but seemed compelled to clarify something. "All the divisions the civilizations appear determined to impose on themselves aren't my doing. When laws, hierarchies and denominations make it easier for groups to keep things running smoothly and everyone on the same page, they serve a purpose, but that's often not the case. Life would have been so much easier if everyone had believed the same things about me, but... oh, well, right?

"Come along, Terry. I think you're going to have a great time broadening your horizons!" God walked Terry to the gates and showed him through.

Terry had just been embraced by God and welcomed to heaven. What a moment! As he joyfully greeted his most beloved family members, it suddenly dawned on Terry that God had side-stepped the Jesus issue. Doggone it, and who knew if he'd ever have another moment with the head honcho?

Weeks (months? years? time is hard to determine in heaven) after being welcomed into heaven by God and, as thrillingly, by family, friends and pets from his life, Terry found himself happening onto an informal chat session.

The group around the table appeared to have recently finished a volleyball game in the adjacent swimming pool. Even though he wasn't dripping wet, he was waved over by one of the group who turned out to be God.

"Terry! Come and meet some new people! How are you doing? Give us a newcomer's perspective." God smiled and pointed out the least wet chair.

"Hi all; thanks for including me," Terry settled in and smiled around the welcoming group, "so I'm the newbie here, huh?"

After a little prodding from people who seemed genuinely interested in hearing his thoughts after his short tenure, Terry opened up and regaled them with his having been mobbed by an exuberant bunch of his beloved dogs. "I had hoped, but never really believed, that I'd see them all again, and it was more joyful than I could have imagined!" Tears flowed from more eyes than his with smiles and nods everywhere. "Of course, the family and friends contingent were a thrill, too, and *they* didn't slobber, either! It's so satisfying to be able to tie up some loose ends in relationships that were left hanging by their deaths. All in all, my welcome to heaven has far exceeded any expectations I'd ever had."

"*That's* what I like to hear!" God laughed. "Eitan here thinks the two of you spoke in the park recently." God indicated the dark-haired fellow on his left.

Terry focused on the man and laughed; "Oh, yes! Sorry, I didn't recognize you with your hair all wet, Eitan." He glanced around the group and added: "We were both considering taking horseback riding lessons, decided 'no' about the same time and took a walk on our own two feet, instead." As the chuckles died down, Terry addressed Eitan again: "You were very patient with my dumb questions and I've given a lot of thought to our conversation; thanks so much for your insights."

"I enjoyed getting to know you, Terry." Glancing around at the others, Eitan explained that Terry had deduced from his name that he was Jewish and had asked if Eitan would be offended if Terry asked a few questions about Judaism and their views on Jesus Christ. "We had a good visit that afternoon. I tried to emphasize that, while we don't believe in Christ or the Trinity, we are totally on-board with God" Eitan paused and nodded in God's direction. "There are as many conflicting teachings in my religion as in any of them, so I kind of look at it as a wash as long as our host here remains the Main Man."

"Hear, hear!" The group happily faux toasted.

"So, tell me, Terry, do you feel more at ease with Eitan and his beliefs that you expected to?" God cheerfully asked.

"Truthfully, while I'm really happy to have made my first Jewish friend and am fascinated by his religion, I'd have to say that I'm even more confused than before about who Jesus actually is. There's always a vagueness in answers about him; or is it just me being dense?"

There was a shifting in chairs and eyes around the table. Finally, God spoke up; "Jesus is, indeed, my son. Just as all of you are my sons and daughters. He's a man who lived an honorable, inspirational life and motivated those in his own time and to this day to believe in God and the hereafter. As a young fellow, Jesus was raised by his fellow man to dizzying heights. I find no fault with his supporters; they were in a fervor of religious joy over who they believed him to be.

"Now, most who have lived beyond their mid-thirties will tell us that they probably learned more from ages 30 to 60 than ever before. Jesus on earth would have, too, given the chance. He was a remarkable young man and deserves our admiration for all he accomplished. As you would expect, he's still a remarkable man! He's never lost his passion for learning and discussing; he is as fascinating as you would imagine him to be."

"He's *here?!*" Almost as one, the group jolted to attention and stared, open-mouthed at God.

"Well, for heaven's sake, where would you *expect* him to be? Yes of course he's here. For obvious reasons, he prefers to keep a low profile and rarely socializes beyond a very small circle, but he's as inspiring a fellow now as he was twenty-one hundred years ago."

"Now, my children, I'm going to excuse myself and get into some dry clothes, shall we meet up in the lounge in an hour or so?" Everyone agreed and God stepped away from the pool area.

After a long, heavy silence, Joan spoke up; "Terry, if you're dense, so am I. While God was speaking, I was transfixed and wondering why I'd never heard the *rest* of the story of before now..." Another voice jumped in: "...He was so open and honest with us, and yet..." "...I know! It's like the definition of 'smoke screen' isn't it?"

After a moment of gathering their thoughts, Terry asked: "Did God Almighty just put all of us on an even plane with Jesus Christ? Surely I mis-heard him."

"If you did, you're not alone!" said Eitan. "Let's all go get dressed before we head for the lounge, shall we?" Everyone concurred and as they reconvened later, God rejoined them. The discussion wasted no time in heating up.

"But it's *called* Christianity! Many religions and churches are literally *named* after him, yet it sounds like you're saying that Jesus isn't the Christ?"

"I may have misspoken, Mario," God began, running a hand through his hair, "What I was trying to say is that Jesus is a wise and loving man; one who made it his earthly calling to make my existence known to his fellow man. The term 'Christ' wasn't affixed to him in his lifetime, you know, but only after his death. 'Christ' is a translation of the word 'Messiah,' and, after his death, Jesus was acknowledged by some to be the Messiah foretold in earlier documents."

"Yes, that's all well and good, but almost everyone I knew had been taught that he was the 'Son of God;' *your* son. In the bible, isn't it in Matthew where you actually claimed him as your son? Are you disavowing him?"

"Not at all! I love Jesus just as I love all of my children but he's not my 'only begotten' son. The whole story of his conception is a delicate one and I wouldn't disparage Mary in any way, she's a good and loving woman and Joseph is as fine a man as there is. But procreation is man's field, not mine. No exceptions.

"As to the new testament and the men who wrote it, they meant well, and they were devoted to Jesus; he *is* an inspirational figure. But, Mario, the first gospel of the new testament was begun forty years after Jesus died. By then, the stories of Jesus, of his death and of those who followed him had reached epic proportions. Please believe me when I tell you that I was not a contributor. It's a fine book but it was written by men who loved and wanted to encourage others to love and revere Jesus. It is all man's doing.

"The old testament, while not my doing either, did foretell the coming of a 'Messiah', but the Jews didn't believe that Jesus was the one." God paused and looked around at the confused faces before continuing.

"Jesus and I have a close relationship and often grapple with the complexities in what religious people on earth are taught. People arrive here expecting to see us sharing a throne. It's awkward for both of us to try to explain that there's only one God and that Jesus of Nazareth is as beloved as they are *and* no more holy than they are.

"Though his followers loved and honored Jesus, they actually led to his death on the cross because several rulers in the Judea area felt so threatened by the devotion of those masses to, basically, an upstart.

"He keeps to his small circle of friends and family because his patience in trying to explain it all has been sorely stretched over two thousand years. I'm glad he has the option and the ability to steer clear of it and be himself."

After a moment's silence, Terry commiserated, "Steering clear of the questions isn't an option *you* have is it? Couldn't you have just wiped all of the jillions of wrong beliefs from our heads before we got here? The same way the hideous earthly experiences many of us endured are only muted, benign and vague memories by the time we get here?"

"Terry, you're new here; I think your fellows who've been here longer would agree that the softening of misplaced beliefs you refer to does occur. Sure, occasional questions pop up about circumcision or some such thing, but they're more a curiosity about why earthly religions chose to do things one way or the other rather than basics about me. I do try to be open about it all and being surrounded by others who have found the truth to be a more palatable look at me and at heaven will probably make it easier for you to let go of your earthly strictures, too."

Eitan leaned forward, "Is it possible... I mean, does Jesus ever talk with any of us? From what you said, it sounds like he doesn't."

"He tends to spend most of his time in an area of heaven populated by his childhood friends and family. Many of the friends of his traveling years have also gravitated there. There's nothing to keep you from going there and seeing if you run into him. Keep in mind, though, that those of Jesus' era arrived here a long time ago and lengthy naps are common. You might get lucky and have a moment with him; he's at least as much in demand with Jews as he is with Christians, though, so don't be disappointed if it's a long line."

With lots of food for thought, but no longer feeling that they weren't hearing the full story about Jesus, the group all thanked God profusely for his time and candor. He laughed and, as they were all rising from their chairs to leave, noted that they were *more* than welcome to share their new insights with everyone they encountered.

***

Worrying About Praying

"Gosh. I can feel you. Am I hallucinating, or are you really here with me? How's it possible that I just know you're here?"

Kelly had been sprawled in the old yard chair with her head thrown back worrying about how to approach God with *this* one.

After she'd thrown a massive, out-of-control temper tantrum on Tuesday, her husband and dog had given her wide berth while they gauged if the worst had passed. This didn't happen very often now that she was officially old, so this one had caught her by surprise.

Finally, last night, Kelly was able to compose herself for a heartfelt apology to her husband Joey. It was graciously accepted and all should have been well. But Kelly could not envision how she was going to approach God about the explosion before attending church on Sunday. Time was running out.

As she now raised her tearful face and looked around, she heard God's voice. "I'm sad that you feel you can't come to me about this" he spoke gently from her soul.

"Oh, God... all I seem to do anymore is beg. I beg you for strength and endurance, for patience, for understanding and on and on. Now, I've behaved abominably and I have to beg forgiveness. I'm exhausted with the begging and I imagine you're fed up with it, too."

"Do you imagine, Kelly, that I don't know the terrible strain you're under? In spite of the fact that your prayers often ask for strength, you always seem to feel *you're* at fault for needing it.

"You are not to blame for Joey's terrible physical and emotional situation. It's not on you that your own precarious health has worsened with the strain of caregiving. All of this will be moot at some point, but while you and Joey are mortal, you have every right to come to your soul for succor."

"But I misbehaved so badly; I was totally out of control. I was mean, vulgar and ugly over *nothing*. Taking a wall-eyed fit over the dog's leash being in the wrong room, for Christ's sake!! Oh, Lord; that's great; swearing in the worst possible way! I'm insane and unforgivable." Breaking into sobs, Kelly's head fell into her hands.

"I try to not be an ogre, Kelly. Whatever it is that you've been told about the 'right' way to pray or the 'respectful' way to approach me, I would like you to know that it isn't my job, or at this juncture, even *possible* for me to blame, reproach and judge you. I want to support you, I want you to come to me for comfort, not cowering in fear that I'll accuse you; you do a bountiful job of that yourself."

"Sounds like you noticed that I couldn't even say a prayer over dinner last night. It would have felt so wrong because I was still so damned mad at the whole world. I was even mad at you, I'm ashamed to say."

"There's the guilt and shame that I'm talking about, Kelly. I get that you wouldn't want to rail at me at the table, but you wouldn't be human if you weren't mad at me sometimes. The world is a vicious and unfathomable mess for you right now. I do get that. Nobody ever said you can't be angry with me about it. But try to do it *without* blaming and shaming yourself."

As the aura of her soul lifted, Kelly took a moment to reflect over all God had spoken. It was a different vision of him than she had harbored for most of her adult life. This was a vision of a lap to curl into when her world and everything in it were simply too great a burden. Of a tender hand to push her hair aside, dry her tears and offer her relief. Could God really be so merciful? Was it possible he wasn't always a disparaging tyrant? Could some of that evaluation of her actually wait until she landed on God's doorstep? What a gift that would be. What a blessing.

***

A Titanic Problem

"**I**'d never before thought to ask if you ever watch movies?" Betsey asked God while trying to adjust her gardening hat with a gloved hand.

God took the moment to lean on his rake. "Sure, I sit in on movie night every once in a while. Why do you ask?"

"Not long before I died, the retirement home where I was living reran Titanic, did you ever see that one?"

"Well, I saw the event it was based on; a horrific occurrence." God began raking up the debris from the bulbs that Betsey and a few others were digging up and dividing. "And I thought the movie did a credible job of portraying the human tragedies involved. What did you think of it?"

"Silly me! Of *course* you knew all about it!" Betsey pulled the huge basket of iris bulbs up onto the bench to work on them. "You know, I'd seen the film when it first came out and was surprised when I sat through it again; I never like movies a second time. But I had thoughts I'd not had when I was younger, and they kept nipping at me. Why do so many of us who profess to believe in you not question why you'd visit the Titanic and Hindenburg catastrophes or school shootings on huge numbers of innocent people? What kind of a being would those acts make you?

"I know you've explained about giving us free choice and a soul to guide us, but most of the people I knew never bothered to put hideous calamities like those into a context that would make us question the 'Will of God' mantra that we'd all been taught from childhood. Why do we have to wait 'til we're here to have it all make sense?"

God propped his rake on a tree and sat in a yard chair across from Betsey. "Boy, girl, if you think that question is puzzling to you, I wish I could tell you how it's bedeviled *me!*

"At some point, as men began trying to make sense of things they didn't understand, they not only acknowledged and named me, but began trying to find ways to accept the unacceptable. They could have just shrugged their shoulders and accepted that, 'stuff happens,' but they complicated it by ascribing *everything* to me. Now, I won't lie to you, there've been times when I happened to be watching as some fool has been speeding on an icy road and ended up in the ditch and I've thought, '*there's* a lesson for you!' But *I* didn't slide that truck into the ditch, physics did.

"Wouldn't you think that a civilization who could come up with physics could come up with better explanations for disasters than 'the will of God?!'" God was exasperated at the end of his tirade.

Betsey had long since laid the pruners in her lap and tried to keep her mouth from gaping as she listened to this rare moment of supreme irritation from God. "Well," she bustled, "we're both going to be in dutch if we don't get this bulb project finished up." She had started to snip in earnest when God spoke up.

"Who's going to come down on *me...?*" he began and then quickly stood and snatched the rake as he realized that neither of them wanted to face Mildred if her gardening schedule wasn't met.

"My dears!" They heard Mildred's cheerful voice just that moment. "Oh, look at all you've gotten done today! Isn't this fun?"

Betsey smiled up at Mildred and agreed. "Wouldn't heaven be boring if we didn't have 'chores' to do? I love that we can do the things like this that were part of our identity on earth."

Mildred jumped in with, "Yet we don't have to do them in nasty weather or if we get a better offer! Yes," she turned to God as he wielded his rake "you planned everything perfectly! Even giving us willing helpers."

"I'm glad you ladies are happy to be here." God chanced a break from the raking, "I've wondered sometimes if, while creating the world, I may have gotten in a bit of a rush to work on heaven and neglected a few things in man's creation."

Betsey clarified for Mildred that she and God had been discussing the fact that his total lack of involvement on earth is so poorly understood before people arrived in heaven.

"Yes, well, I was definitely surprised to find that you *have* no role in earthly matters." began Mildred, "But now I kind of wonder if there's some advantage to having been kept on my toes by so much uncertainty. We would see prayers 'answered' and at least as many totally ignored, so maybe we were prodded into being better people because we just plain didn't know God's reasoning on anything or what the hereafter might hold. The old 'better safe than sorry' thing, dontcha know!"

God promised to give that angle some consideration as the trio began tidying up for the evening.

***

Daddy's Pants

"My daddy couldn't keep his pants zipped," Willa chattered on, "He cheated on Mama right from the beginning, I guess."

"Oh, we three kids knew, as we got older, that daddy had children with a couple of wives after Mama kicked him out. We'd met some of them over the years. But, later, when the internet really got going, we learned of a few other kids who were just plain old bastards. No marriage involved at all."

God was having a hard time keeping the newly arrived Willa focused on the 'Welcome to Heaven' conversation.

Willa launched into another ramble about how many of her father's bastards had come out of the woodwork in the last ten years or so. She'd been diligent about directing them to an online DNA testing site that she'd become all too familiar with; it was shocking, the promiscuity her father had displayed.

"Oh, God," she moaned, "Harry is going to kill me." Her husband Harry was on a fishing trip with some buddies and hadn't yet heard of the home invasion that had resulted in his wife's death.

"Shhh...Willa, my dear woman," God soothed in his most calming voice as he patted her hand. "Do you remember arriving here and having Saint Peter step down from his podium to personally escort you to me? You should be honored; he rarely takes much of a personal interest in anyone. I can't say that I remember this level of confusion in one of my children on their arrival home." His arm snugged the old lady closer to him.

From Willa and Harry's bungalow on earth, the police had called law enforcement in another town to go and notify Willa's daughter of her mother's death and she was on her way back to her childhood home but would be at least a couple of hours before arriving. Their son's phone had gone directly to voicemail and the daughter had told the officer that he could go for days without checking it.

The news of Willa's death was not speeding smoothly among her loved ones or the universe.

Taking advantage of the momentary silence, God, knowing the answer but hoping to re-orient Willa, asked if she had any idea who had broken into her house.

"Well, she didn't exactly break in." Willa sounded sheepish to have to say it; "I'd invited her over for iced tea. She was the latest of Daddy's leftover children to contact me. We'd chatted on the phone enough that I thought that sneaking in a visit while Harry was out of town would be nice."

"So, you're saying the woman who attacked you was a half-sister?" God feigned surprise at this twist.

"I guess so, but she didn't look like a woman, really. I guess there *are* women that tall and muscular, but I was sure surprised when I opened the door. This person was tattooed all over and nothing like what I'd seen in the photo she had emailed me."

God allowed the story to continue in this vein until it began to come back to Willa that the latest person who had passed her DNA requirement for siblinghood had been the last face she'd seen before St. Peter's.

Her husband Harry had cautioned Willa many times over the years about getting too involved with the occasional half-sibling who had shown up online via email or some social media outlet. All of those contacts attested to her father's prodigious philandering and apparent aversion to birth control methods, but those people weren't 'family' just because they shared some DNA, had been Harry's reasoning. Truth be told, this was just the sort of thing he'd feared for his wife.

Now, in God's arms, Willa finally saw the whole picture of her last moments on earth. He made sure the horror she had experienced was expunged, but the finality was there. As she began to regain her composure, God smoothed the hair from her eyes and assured Willa that she was now among her true, forever family and asked if she was ready to be reunited with her older sister, Molly.

"Molly?!" Willa yelped in thrilled astonishment as she permanently forgot her last moments on earth and sprang to her feet. "Molly, Molly, Molly!" she cried as she raced across the room, through the gates and into the open arms of the beloved (and DNA certified) sister running toward her.

***

Champions

"**O**migod!!" Lou was all but jumping up and down in his excitement. "Not only is this the most fabulous golf course I've ever seen anywhere, but I'm in a foursome with God and Arnold Palmer!"

"What am I, chopped liver?" asked the fourth man, Connor, as they waited for God to pull his tee.

"Oh, sorry, man. Really, I didn't mean to dis you..." Lou was interrupted by Connor's high-spirited laughter.

"I'm just pulling your chain, mate, this is the experience of a lifetime, isn't it? I'm as blown away as you are, believe me."

Since neither courses nor schedules are crowded in heaven, the four men were walking this course that put Augusta National to shame. For the moment, God and Arnie seemed in deep discussion, so Connor and Lou were walking together.

As they approached Lou's lie, the other three stepped aside and Connor couldn't resist asking God and Arnold if they had solved all the world's problems in their discussion. The two men chuckled quietly and God said, "Well, not the world's, but maybe *my* problem with a persistent left hook."

Later, in the Nineteenth Hole, Lou asked God, "Conner told me that you and Arnie were working on your left hook; how is it possible that you're not perfect at everything you do? You're God, for heaven's sake."

God laughed and swirled his ice; "Being God doesn't make me perfect, Lou, there are a lot of things that I've never had a chance to experience and, until Arnold got here, golf was one of them. And, of course, sometimes I just mess up on any number of things."

The three others took a few moments to absorb this. Arnie was first to break the silence, "I can tell you, though, that God is a very quick study. When I first got here, I was thrilled to find beautiful and challenging courses and so many world-class players to learn from. When God and I ran into each other again somewhere, he asked if I'd be willing to give him a few lessons so he could see if golf was something he'd be interested in. Now, I'm not much of an instructor, but also not dumb enough to say 'no' to God." Everyone laughed as he continued, "Turns out he enjoyed it and we've played fairly often since then; you two can see that he's a natural and the more he practices the luckier he gets." The two seasoned golfers appreciated Arnie's use of his own well-known quote as praise for God while God himself had to have the compliment explained.

"See?" God followed up, "That's the sort of thing I meant when I said it's totally possible for me to mess up. While, yes, even before the internet, if I *needed* to come up with some bit of trivia - not that anything you say is trivia, Arnie - I could dredge it up, but wouldn't have, and still don't if I don't *have* to... I have a short fuse sometimes, too. I get over it quickly and my default state is pretty cheerful. But, although I can't claim to be 'only human,' I do have my shortcomings."

Connor, who had been in heaven for a bit longer than either Arnold or Lou, spoke up, "For me, God's ownership of his 'imperfections' is one of the things that earned my undying respect for him. I think I'd always imagined him to be an imperious Lord Almighty on a throne with crown and scepter. To find that he's not only willing but eager to experience life's more menial moments, hitting out of a sand trap, playing cards and such, just endeared him to me. And to everyone I've discussed the topic with. When he..." Connor stopped and looked where Palmer and Lou were looking... at God.

And God was trying to not cry.

As he composed himself, God reached over and squeezed Connor's shoulder. "That's one of the finest tributes I've ever received, Connor. Thank you." As Connor began to quibble, God interrupted him, "The fact that you didn't *mean* it as a tribute is what made it so meaningful to me; it was from your soul and genuine. Thank you." God lifted his glass to Connor and the others joined him.

The quiet moment of true camaraderie was savored by the men as the afternoon drew to a close.

***

Running on Full

"I think one of the things that impresses me most about you, Lynne," God continued his conversation with the new arrival, "is that you remained a devout church-goer for all of the sixty-plus years you lived after your accident."

The woman could not stop her pacing with the occasional little hop thrown in just for fun. "Well, I guess you do know that I got awfully angry with you a few times over the years, right?"

"Sure, and understandably so, since, like most people on earth, you would have thought the accident, the wheelchair, being left with paraplegia for life, the unanswered prayers on many topics were all my doing. But, aside from some totally comprehensible anger now and then, you were always loyal to your extensive church family and gave unceasingly to your community."

When this interview began, Lynne had asked God if he would be offended if she kept to her feet and moving for a while. "It's been such a long time since being on my feet was an option for me," she had exulted, "I didn't know what to expect of heaven and am so thrilled to find that walking again really is a part of it! Do you have marathons here? I don't ever want to sit down again!" she had laughed.

Now, though, Lynne did take the chair across from God. "I couldn't have done it by myself, you have to know that. I was blessed to be placed in the world's best rehab center after the accident. They helped my family to help me and we all came away from that beginning with the tools we'd need to deal with it every day for the rest of my life." She paused and her eyes showed tears. "And Davie, Oh, God, I have thanked you every day for that man. He was the handsomest young Marine you have ever seen when we met a few years after the accident, and I swear, it was love at first sight. He saw me, not the big, shiny crutches, but *me.* He is a born caregiver and was totally undaunted by what life with me would mean." Lynne swallowed the tears and put her shoulders back in pride. "We had a few naysayers, but we never looked back."

"No, you didn't. You and Dave made more differences in more lives than either of you ever realized. You both came from broken homes yet persevered in your marriage. You both really epitomize the lemons/lemonade saying. Your kindnesses, positivity and caring for children, elders and everyone in between were just exceptional.

"Do you have any idea how many people consider you to be a hero of major proportions?" God asked the lovely woman facing him.

"Me?! Why...what on earth would make you think such a thing?"

"Well, have you ever tried to look at your own life objectively? Trying to see yourself from others' viewpoints?" God didn't even try to keep the smile from his own amazed face.

"Oh. I guess you mean because of my disability. I sure hope there was more to me than *that*! Gosh, I was married to the same man for 66 years, raised great kids and helped with my grandkids. As you said, we were always active in our church and in the senior home where my mother spent her last years. Davie and I kept a bible study group alive by sheer determination and stayed active in Al-Anon, helping others to overcome their families' addictions. There was so much more to my life that that stupid wheelchair.

"Oh, and I was blessed to have seen so much of the world, too!" Lynn enthused, "Davie and I loved cruises with our friends and family and he never let my disability keep us from going places!"

"And you don't consider that to be 'hero' material? You've just made my point for me, Lynne. Most people made paraplegic at eighteen do not go on to sixty-six-year marriages to someone they didn't even know before the accident. Nor to all of the other things you accomplished. You had a zeal for life that inspired you to keep yourself healthy by using crutches for as long as you could, by playing sports and by swimming until the last week of your life. You pretty much redefined 'determination.'

"I wish I had some above-average reward here for you, but I know that you'll make every minute special for yourself and everyone you come into contact with.

"Hey!" sang God as he accompanied Lynne toward the magnificent gates, "How would you like to take my personal little back gate into heaven? You see the big pearlies right there, and if you ever want to come back and actually walk through them, just let Peter know. But I'd like to share with you something that's just mine. Welcome to heaven, Lynne!" God called after her as she hurdled over the short decorative gate and ran like the wind through the glorious green expanse and toward all the loved ones waiting at the finish line.

***

The Soul of the Matter

"So, you're saying you created the heavens, the earth and everything on it. Yet, you retained no control over the evolving situation for yourself? You just swiped your hands together and went home?"

This was the second time in only a few days that God had found himself in a conversation with someone who wanted to delve deeper into God's involvement with earthly matters. Mitch had been here in heaven for some time and was always an interesting fellow to chat with, but it was usually about fishing; which the two were doing today from the bank of a wide, meandering stream.

"Basically, yes. I returned here to be sure heaven was going to be a delightful, stimulating eternity for those who earned it. And you wouldn't believe the bookkeeping nightmare it is to keep up with every deed and misdeed by every person alive. I have a system, of course, and it doesn't include yellow legal pads, but for now, they're something that everybody recognizes as a note-taking tool. So I use them as a point of reference."

"Wow," said Mitch, "I never even thought of how you keep track of all that!"

"Luckily, I was able to transition from stone tablets to laptops pretty easily, but it's still time-consuming work. The part of the job I really love are the interactions with all of the people here, it's a joy to me. But the hard part is trying to convince them that I wasn't ignoring their prayers for all those years and making life hard just for the entertainment value of it.

"You've heard the old saw that 'God helps those who help themselves?' Well, that pretty much describes what my plan for the soul was; I wanted people to make their own way while knowing I was a part of them. It was never my intent to macro-manage every detail of every life or the weather.

"The only bit of myself I left with him was his soul; a certainty he could use to balance right and wrong, heaven and hell. A moral compass."

God and Mitch both happened to be reeling in at the same time and took a few quiet minutes to check their bait and re-cast.

"But then, why are we taught from the ground up to pray to you for guidance, mercy or a good crop? If you can't reroute a hurricane or save a drowning man, why do we all cry out to you so instinctively?"

"Religion." stated God with an edge to his voice. "While ancient people were finding their footing, their souls told them I existed and they struggled to find ways of sharing and exploring that knowledge with each other. Temples started out as gathering places to discuss what each person felt and imagined about me. When differences of opinion arose, there began to be different religions and sects of belief. But when something becomes so powerful, it will get abused by those *seeking* power."

"But, couldn't you have stopped it? Or made everyone believe the same thing about you?"

"Nope. My work on earth was long finished. I had no influence by then. Except for those souls I'd left with all of you."

"So," persisted Mitch, "when will life on earth end? When I left ten years ago, people were already saying that Armageddon. the End Times, the Rapture or whatever, was imminent. Is there a timeline?"

"You know," mused God, "I'm usually a pretty good conversationalist, but I've sure been striking out on this topic lately. I think the world down there has gotten so complicated in the last hundred years that the term 'natural order' has lost its resonance. Many people have never been out of a city, their lives are reliant on technology that is bound to fail them, and they're torn in too many directions. I certainly didn't put an expiration date on it when I put the world into being, but you're right, it looks grim right now. Man has not handled his gifts very responsibly.

"I'd love to be able to help, but I can't. All I can do is offer some peace and joy when they get here."

***

Eighth, Ninth and Tenth Commandments
You Shall Not Steal, Lie or Cover
Bam!

The last few months of poker nights, with no discussion of commandments, had felt like old times and everyone was cheerful and relaxed as they tidied up after tonight's game. They all chose comfy chairs to continue the lighthearted discussion they'd been having over the last hand.

The group had all been laughing about the squirrel who had put on a show in the park last week by stealing a dog's tug toy and racing up a tree with it. The goofy squirrel had found a crotch in the oak, turned around to face the dog and set up a loud, taunting chatter.

"That poor dog was beyond frustrated at having his toy stolen!" laughed Ruby.

Carl chuckled "Guess those animals never heard of the eighth commandment!" It was no more out of his mouth than Carl's eyes got wide and he cringed as he looked at Fausto and Ruby.

After a short silence, God asked, "Okay, what did I miss? I feel like the odd man out, here."

Fausto began "...Well, sir..." He was laughingly interrupted by God.

"*Sir!* Oh, this must be serious! I don't remember any of you three calling me 'sir' since, *maybe,* your first day here, if that. What's going on?"

"Guys, I think we've been caught." Ruby looked from Carl to Fausto and asked, "Shall I fess up?" Their hangdog nods told her to have at it.

"Gosh, this is awkward. Do you remember the last time we had a 'commandments' discussion; a few months ago? After you left," she addressed God, "we stumbled into a conversation admitting that we really weren't enjoying the ten commandment chats as much as we'd anticipated. We all felt, and, I guess especially in light of your unease over one of your children that night, that too many of the commandment talks had been discomfiting to all of us. Have they seemed that way to you?"

God, in his characteristic way, rumpled his hair as he came up with an answer. "You three never cease to surprise me. Yes, I noticed that some of those talks have felt a little ouchy for some reason, but I guess I thought you all saw them as consequential. For me, the commandments are kind of a moot point; they're not bad advice, but they weren't something I handed down, so I feel pretty detached from their significance."

"But you were willing to participate just to make us happy." Fausto spoke up. "That is so *you*. Really, even if you weren't God, I'd have to say that you're one of the nicest guys I've ever known."

God laughed as they all concurred with Fausto. "Okay, then, how do we wrap this thing up and put it to bed? Did you three come up with a plan?"

"Well," Carl began, "we did mention the possibility of rolling the last three into a quick and dirty one and done. I'm all for it, but whatever works for the rest of you is fine by me."

"Okay, then," Fausto jumped in, "That scoundrel squirrel should have *known* that it's not right to steal!" Everyone laughed and applauded before Rose exuberantly added, "And he shouldn't go home and lie to his mother by bearing false witness and trying to pin it on the dog!"

Whoops of approval went through the group. Carl jumped in to add "I hope the poor thing learned to not covet, since the toy ended up falling to the ground, anyway."

"Bam!! Huzzah! You guys did it! You got us all out of the sticky wicket and we finished with a bang!" God was exhilarated as they all laughed and made fun of themselves and the situation they'd gotten into. Poker nights promised to get back to normal.

***

<u>GATES</u>

"Wait...aren't you the one who spent years flippantly saying you couldn't believe in a God who had no sense of humor? Or who had a thin skin?" came the voice.

"Yes, that's me" you answer, confident that St. Peter is preparing to wave you right through to your interview with God on this glorious, light-filled morning.

"*Your* God was too busy with important things to take major offense at swearing, right?" Peter's voice had risen alarmingly "He wouldn't have given you the ability to enjoy ice cream, sex and horse-racing if he was going to damn you *for* enjoying them, wasn't that your reasoning?"

Pete steps from behind his imposing podium as sudden thunderclouds and lightning produce a deafening, blinding maelstrom that envelops you both. His face has gone dark and wrathful, his fingers are flashing bolts of energy. Robes whipping furiously around him, eyes so fierce you can't meet them, he roars in a voice that overwhelms the storm: "You imbecile!! Who did you think you were dealing with?! Who did you think those commandments were directed at if not at your prideful, sinning, insignificant self?!"

"But...but..." you sputter, ducking your head and hunching your shoulders to avoid a blast from the howling tumult.

"Nothing!! Not one word from your sniveling mouth!" Peter bellows. "God Almighty will hear your mewling excuses and you will know the meaning of fury!"

You've gone through life grateful to a God whose requirements of you so nicely conformed to the parameters by which you chose to live it. He has expected you to be respectful of others, generous to those less fortunate than you, kind to all living things and other guidelines that really haven't proven to be too onerous.

And now this?! Sheesh, how much worse could Hell be than this onslaught of wrath from both nature and a fellow whose state of being is unclear? Is he human? Divine? And... wait!... what is he doing now?! Good God in Heaven! He's become a whirling dervish who seems to envelop all of heaven, hell and earth. You're swirled into it like strawberries into a blender...the howl is horrific... and then it stops.

You're afraid to look up from your facedown sprawl on the ground...or whatever the surface is. Are you in one piece? If nothing else, the silence is blessed. And then it's broken by a voice you don't recognize... "Wow, I see you caught Peter on a theatrical tear; he's a wild man, isn't he?" Your confidence long gone, you have no idea how to respond; is it even you being addressed? Is it a rhetorical question? Are there others included in the query? You reluctantly peep up to see an aura of calm, kind of a warm, undefined glow.

Raising your head higher, you see a guy who is the spitting image you've always held of God: long white hair and beard, intense eyes and billowing white robes.

"You can get up; things have calmed down" he says. The voice is surprisingly...human; gentle even. What's the protocol here? Is this even God or another one of his unpredictable minions? Once on your feet, should you bow? Grovel? This is uncharted territory.

Trying, as you rise, to straighten the 'Sunday Best' garb you were buried in, you're asked to take a seat. The two of you appear to be in a meandering, storybook park with inviting benches under sun-dappled trees. The place is comfortably shabby, not manicured to perfection but fully delightful. Choosing a metal armchair with peeling turquoise paint, you sit and wonder.

"So... Saint Peter tells me you have an attitude," the man (or whatever) says conversationally. "Now, don't get defensive about that, I'm just trying to get a handle on you. You seem to have lived a pretty decent life," he mused as he scanned some notes on a yellow pad. "None of the automatic disqualifiers here, but no mind-boggling heroics, either. Not that those are required; I realize life is like running a gauntlet just to stay decent. But why don't you tell me what makes you think I'm not a stickler for adherence to religious guidelines?"

"Um, well, Sir...gosh, I'm so nervous. I don't want to be a smart aleck, but I'd have to ask which denomination you're referring to?"

The silence is benign but unbroken.

"Religion always just confused me, Sir. There are so many of them and most don't agree on much. Some church groups rewrite their texts because the members don't agree with each other on what the Bible actually says or means. It doesn't seem like it should be that complicated, if you see what I mean."

Left to flounder in the stillness, you try another tack. "Did you actually tell those people what to write in the Bible? Did the Commandments really just appear on Earth? Is Jesus really your son, or was he as human as I am?" After each question, there's been no response, so you keep digging the hole deeper.

"Faith seemed so much simpler when I was a kid; my parents told me: God expects this or that and so do we. It was basic: be kind and pay your own way. I haven't always nailed it, but my life was happier and less complicated when I did.

"I really apologize if I made you feel disrespected by not adhering to any one religion's criteria; insulting you was never my intention, Sir."

The big guy replies: "If you are admitted to heaven, what are your dreams and expectations?"

"Oh. Wow. Well, I guess the thing I hope for the very most is to be reunited, in whatever form you choose, Sir, with all of the loved ones from my life. To let them know how much I've missed and loved them every day and how important they were to me. I was careless in so many cases about letting them know how loved they were when I had the chance."

After a long pause and receiving a searing once-over, you begin to think your goose is cooked. You imagine having the funeral attire licked off your body by the flames of Hell. You mourn the loss of your loved ones all over again. You wonder what you could have done to better show your love of and respect for God.

Then...Poof! God has hugged you and opened a pair of magnificent pearly gates for you. The light blinds you for a moment before you begin to see the magical garden populate with all of your favorite people and pets. They're all full of love for you and joy at your arrival.

There is a Heaven. There is a God.
Glory Hallelujah!

***

Afterword

Of course, I have no more clue than anyone else has about God, heaven or hell. But I'm not afraid to admit it and explore some of the contradictions we've all encountered from childhood on.

I've had stretches of time when I wore a cross at my neck and stretches when God rarely crossed my mind. I've always believed in God but was never a regular churchgoer or bible devotee. The 'community' aspect of church seems more important today than ever; we're all scattered in too many directions and having that core group must be comforting.

Sporadically, over about twenty-five years, I was an in-home Hospice volunteer. I saw people at their worst, their most inspirational and everything in between. It was one of the most enriching experiences of my life. Then, after the painful and religiously frustrating death of a dear friend, I decided I was going to have to get real with myself and see what my actual beliefs were about God.

It turned out to be a simpler task than I had anticipated. Writing it down began as a months-long, personal Q&A exercise to clarify my beliefs for myself, but I found such fun and peace in it that I wanted to share.

The God who has settled in my heart created a dizzyingly disparate people to populate the earth and I see him as perfectly able to be in every soul at the same time and with the ability to be what each person needs him to be in that moment. I've come to believe that God is a crucial, living part of us through our souls. That our prayers, thanks and admonitions are live conversations with this bit of God available to us whenever we take a moment to consult him. Not that he grants or ignores prayers, but that he helps us to take counsel from our souls and find the strength to handle whatever comes.

I live in an area too often impacted by forest fires. Recently, as the wind gusts reached 50mph, I found myself starting a knee-jerk prayer regarding the simmering situation outside. Then, rather than *ceasing* the prayer, I found myself in consultation with my own soul about whether our go-bags and other preparations were up-to-date and whether any needed to be reviewed.

It was a perfect illustration of how examining what can actually be *done* in a situation is so much more calming and empowering for me than flinging out a prayer with little likelihood of its being answered. And then feeling betrayed when it isn't.

Getting to know God has enriched my life. I hope God's Poker Night has either solidified your relationship with him or offered you some food for thought. Thanks for reading.

***

Reader reviews are the lifeblood
of self-published authors.
Yours on Amazon, Goodreads or
others would be greatly
appreciated.

CPSIA information can be obtained
at www.ICGtesting.com
Printed in the USA
JSHW022047080222
22725JS00004B/31